MW01171371

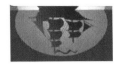

The Missing Christmas Card

By

Joan Byrd

Deep Indigo Books

Published by Indigo Sea Press
Winston-Salem

Deep Indigo Books
Indigo Sea Press
302 Ricks Drive
Winston-Salem, NC 27103
This book is a work of fiction. Names, characters,
locations and events are either a product of the author's
imagination, fictitious or used fictitiously. Any resemblance
to any event, locale or person, living or dead, is purely
coincidental.

For information regarding bulk purchases of this book,
digital purchase and special discounts, please contact the publisher
at indigoseapress@gmail.com

Cover Design by Pan Morelli
Manufactured in the United States of America
ISBN 978-1-63066-549-4

I dedicate this book to Patrick, my amazing guardian angel, whose God-given gift of storytelling and my God-given gift of writing has blessed this world with many beautiful books, all different, all page-turners. Learn more about my beloved friend on the final pages of the book at:
Author's Notes.

—Joan Byrd

CHAPTER 1

December 22, 1814

The big fancy carriage had started out early from the elaborate mansion sitting high on a hill overlooking the small town of Sleepy Creek. Most of the town and a thousand acres surrounding the town, belonged to its founder, William Marshall and his wife Susanne.

Mr. Avery Torrance, the carriage driver, was given the title: the family chauffer and he was part of a small friendly staff that enjoyed working for the Marshall's and their ten-year-old daughter, Pattie. Instead of having separate quarters on the grounds for the staff, the kind couple considered their employees family and gave them their own accommodations in the big house's west wing. So, the entire west wing consisted of nine faithful staff members. Mable Folly, the jolly cook, Clarence Rockford, the British butler, twin sisters, Milly and Tilly Shields, the cleaning staff, the Marshall's personal maids, Rose Redding, Velda Turner, and Joyce Ann Goodyear, Pattie's personal maid. The ninth employee was Lucas Peppers, the gardener and Avery Torrance's best friend.

The kind carriage driver never questioned different changes in the Marshall's busy routine, no matter how strange they seem to him. Such as it was this very morning when Susanne Marshall would be stuck behind her big desk in the book-filled library, getting out the Marshall Mill's employee's payroll, making sure each worker got his Christmas bonus. Then she must finish the end of the year reports and place an order for new rolls of material, enough string to start the new year, the long strips of fancy lace that made the lady's long night gowns so appealing to their many customers. Besides the night gowns, the big mill produced, men's clothing, like flannel work shirts, dress shirts, overalls, dress pants, overcoats for

1

men, women and children of all ages. Also, for the lady of the house, winter and summer day dresses, Sunday attire, plus useful things for the home, towels, curtains and bed linens. So, instead of making her usual orders for reopening after the holidays, Susanne ask the carriage driver to hook up the carriage and escort her and her daughter, Pattie to the Russel Farm, about five miles from Sleepy Creek.

Turning the four white horses down the narrow country road that led to the outskirts of town, Avery's smooth handling of the gentle horses made the ride down the uneven road seem smooth to Susanne Marshall and Pattie and he could tell by the gentle hum of the wheels that both passengers where relaxed and enjoying the beautiful country setting they rode beside.

Doing his job well had led the Marshall family to respect Mr. Torrance and they considered him a part of their extended family. Even though Avery Torrance came highly recommended by a previous respective friend of William Marshall, the owner of Marshall Mills refused to rush in on the decision to hire Torrance right away without first checking out his work and willingness to take orders. Usually the mild-mannered man, William had been unhappy with his first two carriage drivers, neither of which lasted more than a few weeks. His first driver drove reckless, running the big wheels on and off the road, jarring the passengers around until Susanne caught him drinking down a bottle of rum before climbing in the driver's seat. The obnoxious second driver hated taking orders from Mr. Marshall and refused to brush down the horses before putting them up with feed and fresh water. So, after a heated argument between boss and worker, the irate man was fired.

So, to prove himself good at his job, Avery Torrance had worked for William Marshall four years and got the reward he had worked so hard for, to send for his wife and two children, who had also sacrificed the same four years without a husband and father.

The white farmhouse came into view as the friendly driver called back to his silent companions. "Mrs. Marshall, I shall be

2

pulling the carriage up at the Russel's front door madam, then I will help you and Miss Pattie down before I gather your packages from the back."

"Thank you, Mr. Torrance. The ride out this morning was quite pleasant despite the winter chill in the air." Susanne Marshall held out her hand for his gentlemanly assistance in helping her from the high carriage. Having a daughter of his own, Avery felt very close to the Marshall girl and his eyes twinkled with fatherly love as he helped her down.

"I will see to those beautiful Christmas gifts now." After retrieving the two wrapped gifts from the storage rack in the back of the carriage, the driver gently placed them in mother and daughter's outstretched hands. "I am certain the Russel's will love such beautifully wrapped presents. I know my Charlotte and little Fannie would be delighted just from the pretty wrappings."

"Mr. Torrance, I know it cannot be easy to be separated from your beautiful family for so long and to miss all those special occasions that come along, such as birthdays, wedding anniversaries, and Christmas." Susanne knew of her husband's reluctance in hiring another driver right away after the first two proved bad apples. "And now another Christmas has arrived and you are still spending your holidays apart"

"Apart yes, but with the hope of being together at last this coming spring at last." Avery Torrance was not a person to drag everyone down because of his situation so he always tried to turn a negative into a positive."

"Avery, I cannot wait to meet Fannie and Evan." Pattie gave him her beautiful angelic smile. "If they take after their papa they have to be terrific children."

"That is very sweet of you to say Miss Pattie and coming from you I take it as a wonderful compliment." The soft-spoken driver gave them a slight bow. "I shall wait by the horse's madam."

"Thank you, Mr. Torrance, we shouldn't be long." Susanne straightened the bow on the gift in her hand, then reached over to tidy up her daughters. "We were going to wait until Christmas church service to give our gifts, but Pattie insisted I bring her over this morning before I got busy with my office work. Her gift to Hattie just could not wait another second." She gave Pattie a loving pat on her cheek. "Let's go and deliver our gifts, then return home."

Avery noticed the young girl's sad face drop in disappointment, her petite fingers clutching the gift lovingly. "Pattie, Hattie Russel will love anything you give her. I've never seen two better friends than the two of you."

Pattie glanced up and gave him a sweet smile. "Thank you. Avery. I have got to stay long enough to see her face when she opens this gift."

"I'm sure your mama will give you a little time with your friend. Now stop fretting and run catch your mama before she knocks on the Russel's door." Avery gave a soft chuckle as he watched the young girl move swiftly to catch up with her very proper mother. The drivers smooth hand ran gently down one of the horse's strong neck as he spoke softly. "Good girl, Heather. We shall stand back and watch the giving of both the gift and love shared between those precious little girls.

"Mrs. Marshall and Pattie, what a lovely surprise to see you both this morning. Please, come in and warm up by the fire." Mrs. Russel never let unsuspecting visitors bother her busy morning routine. She genuinely loved everyone, stranger or friend. Hattie ran up beside her mother when she heard her friend's name, wiping off the chocolate from her lips. Her mother smiled down at her excited daughter. "Please forgive my cookie tester, but the chocolate cookies just came out of the oven and there is plenty, if you both can join us."

"That is most gracious of you, Margaret, but we never intended to barge in on you right here before Christmas. The reason for our early morning visit was for my daughter to bring your daughter her present. Pattie simply insisted it could not wait because it was something she wanted Hattie to have before the holidays were over."

"Then it must be important to Pattie to give Hattie her gift now." Margaret reached for Hattie's coat and scarf, then helped her daughter in them. "Hattie, it's a beautiful morning and the swing is in the warm sun. Why don't you take your friend out there while I visit with Susanne a few minutes?"

"Thanks mama!" Hattie grabbed her friend's hand and walked swiftly toward the swing. The friendly farm girl waved at the coachman. "Good morning, Avery! How is your day going so far?"

"My day could not be better, Miss Hattie Russel." The driver gave her a genuine smile. "Seeing your cheerful happy face does make a heart feel good! Thank you for asking."

"If you like cookies, Avery, my mama just baked another two dozen chocolate cookies this morning." Hattie and Pattie reached the swing and flopped down, their attention still on the friendly man. "Would you like some to take with you for later?"

"Miss Hattie Russel, I would love a couple of those cookies if it's alright with your mama." The driver climbed back up to sit down, knowing the girls wanted to talk and knew Susanne Marshall would make her visit brief. "Go on with your visit girls while I rest my eyes." Never meaning to ease drop on the friend's conversation, Avery Torrance remained quiet, pretending to be napping while taking in every word they spoke.

Hattie could not stop looking down at the beautifully wrapped present in her friend's hand. "Pattie, this is a real surprise. I thought we agreed to exchange our gifts at the Christmas service. Why did you need to give it to me so early?"

"Dear friend, I would hardly call December 22 early! In three more days it will be Christmas." Pattie reached for her best friend's hand. "Hattie, I just could not wait to give you my gift so you could start using it right away!" She laid the pretty package in her friend's lap. "Please open it now, my dear friend, before mama comes from your house. I will have to leave."

5

Joan Byrd

Hattie's fingers ran over the exquisite gift, adorned with a big bow. "Gee Pattie, it's almost too pretty to unwrap." Noticing the anxious look on her friend's beautiful face, Hattie began removing the rich paper slowly, in hopes to save it to use on the gift she would give Pattie. "I feel really bad about not having your gift ready yet, Pattie. Daddy gets paid at the mill on Friday so I cannot go shopping until Saturday morning. I really want to get you something very special."

"Hattie, you need not explain. Your friendship means the world to me, so whatever you give me will be cherished for as long as I live." Pattie's bright laughter from watching her friend's big eyes when she opened the lid, made the coach driver glanced their way to see Hattie holding up a beautiful new diary with Hattie Russel engraved on the top in pure gold.

Avery got caught up in the girl's excitement when she let out a delightful burst of laughter and grabbed Pattie in a tight hug, giving her best friend continuing thanks.

"Now Hattie, we both have a diary to write down all our special times together, starting with today!" Pattie laughed as her friend grabbed her in another grateful hug. "I'm glad you like it! There's ink and a quill pen down in the box!"

"You thought of everything! I absolutely love it Pattie! It is the best gift I have ever received!" Hattie took a big breath.

"There is one gift better, my friend! The very first Christmas gift ever given."

"Yes, there is Pattie! There will never be a gift as great as the one our heavenly Father gave us. Jesus our Savior!" Hattie smiled up and blew out grateful kisses toward the heavens.

Mr. Torrance couldn't help but smile as he watched the good friends showing pure innocent love. It made him think of is own children he had left behind to come get this steady job he had needed so badly to take care of his family. Fannie, now eight and his son, Evan, age ten. Avery tried to picture how the children looked now, four years after he saw them last at four and six. Glancing down at his hand, he smiled at the simple wedding band he cherished so dearly. Avery could still see his

6

shy wife as she slipped the ring on his finger and how beautiful she looked on their wedding night. Reaching inside his vest pocket, the carriage driver pulled out the last letter his Charlotte had sent him. He would read it a tenth time.

"Dearest Avery, it is hard to think we must be separated yet another Christmas, but your last correspondence gave me hope. At long last, your dear employer, William Marshall has finally realized what a devoted worker you are and now considers you one of his permanent staff members. The cottage you have described that Mr. Marshall is having built just for our family, already sounds like home, my darling. You are there and we shall all be together at long last.

I cannot believe it has been four years since we were together. I suppose to lose two drivers within the first year of moving to Sleepy Creek made Mr. Marshall extra cautious choosing a coachman. It had to be hard on you to leave little four-year-old Fannie and six-year-old Evan, who you were training the first steps of horse grooming. As for you and I, dear husband, I know you miss me as much as I miss you and long to be together again.

"I do cherish all your beautiful letters throughout the year, but it is that special Christmas card you pick out for me each Christmas that I look most forward to. The children are excited about their own personal Christmas cards again this year and you might be surprise how far the dollar placed in their cards can stretch. I am overjoyed that we can spend next Christmas together, dearest Avery. Until then, stay safe, stay well and try to enjoy your Christmas. The children and I send our love and miss you. Your Charlotte."

Avery sat up when he heard the screen door shut and the sound of women's voices. "Thank you for the beautiful linen tablecloth for me to needlepoint, Susanne. It shall grace my dining room table next Christmas." Margaret Russel smiled over at her daughter, obviously happy over the gift her friend Pattie brought her. "Girls, finish your talk. Mrs. Marshall needs to get back."

"Margaret, thank you again for boxing up these cookies. I have never seen such a variety of beautiful Christmas cookies." Susanne's attention fell on the two girls hugging as they walked toward them. "Margaret, do you think Hattie could have a sleep over tonight with Pattie?" Hattie froze in her steps as she listened to Pattie's mother. "This is such a busy time for both me and the staff, sometimes Pattie seems left out. I am sure she would love having her best friend over for a night."

Mrs. Russel noticed the anxious expression on her daughter's face and she felt sure the girl was holding her breath by the pink flush growing on her cheeks. "Susanne, that is very thoughtful of you. I think Hattie would love to spend the day and night with Pattie. Wouldn't you, Hattie?"

"Yes, ma'am!" Hattie almost jumped out of her coat as she grabbed Pattie. "Did you here your mama ask my mama if I could have a sleep in with you tonight?"

"What did your mama say?" Pattie grew excited over the idea.

"She said I could go! I best run in and pack my things!" Hattie raced up the steps and stopped briefly to offer her gratitude. "Thanks a million, Mrs. Marshall! I will pack fast!"

"I better give Hattie a hand, Susanne and get her out to the carriage." Margaret watched the driver climbing from the high carriage, then followed her daughter up to her room.

Hattie came out in less than ten minutes changed, a better coat, a cloth travel bag and four cookies wrapped up for Avery Torrance.

CHAPTER 2

Avery Torrance had waited for the Marshall family to enjoy their dinner with Pattie's young guest, Hattie Russel. After having desert, the small group went into the music room to enjoy listening to Susanne Marshall play a few Christmas carols on a fine grand piano. Then the friends were excuse to go up to Pattie's room just to chat or play with some of her many beautiful dolls.

The quiet chauffeur had been sitting just inside the Marshall's big library, half reading and half listening to muffled conversation, mostly by the girls and Susanne Marshall. William had rarely spoken two words throughout the five-course meal. The once happy man seemed irritated and moody and when Avery delivered Mr. Marshall to his office in town, he would jump at every small bump in the road or yell out at a pedestrian who got in the way of his carriage. Once he was let off, his sudden burst of temper led him to shove anyone who might cross his path out of his way.

Before William Marshall had become so irrational, Avery could ask him for some stationary to write his letter to his wife Charlotte, but ever since his last outburst over the request, he decided to ask Susanne Marshall for the stationary instead. So, this was his reason for waiting in the library for the mistress of the mansion. Susanne returned every night to her work desk which sit in the far corner of the large room. It was here she wrote her own letters or address the Marshall's many Christmas cards. Avery felt sure Susanne would give him a few sheets.

While the patient chauffeur waited, he heard the sound of familiar voices just outside the library door in the big hallway that ran the length of the grand mansion. It was the soft voice of William Marshall and the distinctive British accent of

Clarence Rockford, the house butler.

"Listen Rockford, I told you I would give you my answer tonight, outside, twelve sharp! Not in here! Not now!"

"Then I suggest that you show up tonight, twelve sharp! In the rose garden!" Mr. Rockford sounded harsh, demanding, as though he was the one in charge, not his employer. "He will not like your disobedience again William Marshall! When you make a bargain with him you may not altar your course! Do I make myself clear?"

"I will be there, for God's sake! Just leave me!" Hearing footsteps moving swiftly in different directions, silence filled the hallway as Avery Torrance grew tense, not sure what Mr. Marshall had gotten himself into. The possibility of some kind of danger for the gentle man he looked up to and admired ever since he first met him four-years-ago, was too obvious. Then it occurred to him that this danger could involve his wife, Susanne and his angelic daughter, Pattie. With the entire staff living in quarters, everyone within these beautiful walls may be a part of this 'bargain' Rockford spoke of. Feeling a part of the loving family and fellow workers gave the carriage driver a new sense of protector. So, he would keep his eyes on Clarence Rockford and find out just what he was up to and who this powerful man was who seemed to be the one in charge.

"I will try to stay up tonight and see for myself just who this man is making my employer's life so miserable "Avery whispered to himself. "My room faces the rose garden and with the moon almost full, I will be able to make out the men standing below my window." He grew quiet when Susanne Marshall walked in the library and gave the friendly family man a big smile.

"It makes me feel good to know a few of our loyal workers enjoy reading, Avery." Susanne continued her conversation as she walked back to her desk. "I know you are wanting to write your letter to Charlotte and I find that very loving." She waved him over to her desk as she opened one of the big drawers and took out a new box of stationary with matching envelopes. "I

10

couldn't help but hear the conversation between you and William when you ask him for some stationary." Susanne's eyes held sadness as she handed the carriage driver the beautiful box and laid some stamps on top. "Avery, I must apologize for my husband. He hasn't been himself lately, as I'm sure you are aware. I know he offered to give you as much stationary as you needed to write your wife when you first arrived. Up until lately William happily gave you all you required."

"Mrs. Marshall, there is no need to explain. I just pray Mr. Marshall can find some peace over whatever he is going through." Avery's eyes misted up "I genuinely care about all of you and just wish the best years are yet to come for all who live within these walls." He glanced down at the beautiful box of stationary, still filled with emotion. "This is enough stationary to write my Charlotte several letters. I sincerely thank you."

"You are more than welcome Avery. I just wish you did not have to spend another Christmas without your family, but by the next holiday season, you should be happily spending Christmas in your own home with Charlotte and your children." Susanne looked thoughtful for a moment, then added. "Tell me, have you sent your usual Christmas cards off yet? To mail it now might mean receiving late cards."

"I mailed the children their cards six days ago. My daughter Fannie's is a festive picture of Santa Clause and Evan will appreciate the proud reindeer with garland and holly on his antlers." Mr. Torrance made a helpless face. "As for Charlotte's card, I just haven't found the perfect card for her yet. I know how special they are to her and so far, the first three Christmas cards pleased her greatly, but I simply cannot find that right card for her."

"Maybe I can help you with that perfect card, Avery." Taking a key from her dress pocket, Susanne Marshall opened a secret door and pulled out a red box. "I found these beautiful cards in a little gift shop while visiting friends in New York.

They were so unique and different from any card I had ever seen. All the cards inside this box are different and came with just art on the front. To make the card personal and distinctly your own, the artist placed a drawing of me and William, along with our dog Rusty. Pattie had not been born when I made the purchase." Susanne opened the fancy lid and picked up the first card. "The cards are numbered and dated Christmas, 1803. I think number one is the perfect Christmas card for Charlotte. The title of this edition is: The Welcome Home Set, so, what could be more appropriate for her knowing she will be coming to her new home soon." Susanne handed the happy man the card he had hoped to find.

Looking down at the perfect card, Avery saw a couple dressed in their finest Christmas clothes, standing outside a Christmas house, facing the front door. The words written below read simply, A Merry Christmas To You! The big green door opened and the same couple are standing at the entrance being greeted by William and Susanne Marshall, along with the family dog, Rusty. Avery Torrance thanked the gracious lady and walked up to his room, knowing he had the perfect card for his Charlotte.

Even with Avery Torrance's good intentions to remain awake until the dreaded meeting in the rose garden, the long day's workload had worn out the carriage driver. He tossed and turned as bad dreams invaded his restless sleep. The striking of the big grandfather clock down in the main hall brought him awake.

"Twelve chimes." He spoke just above a whisper and sat up and noticed the soft rays of moonlight glowing around the room. Avery's body seemed frozen in bed, his mind racing with questions. Was Mr. Marshall, the man he looked up to with devotion, down in the rose garden at this ungodly hour, meeting with Clarence Rockford and some stranger who seemed to hold his employer's life in his hands.

Finding the strength, the thoughtful man slipped from the covers and into his slippers. He made his way slowly to the darkest side of the window to keep from being seen below, then gently cracked it open, hoping to hear what was said. Avery could see the garden plainly in the full moonlight as he watched the owner of the house walk out to the middle and began speaking to something invisible. Even though the strange transaction between his employer and some invisible being, Avery felt safe watching from his dark window on the top floor. "Maybe Mr. Marshall is praying." He thought for a moment until he saw the butler walk out to join the invisible thing and start talking.

"So, William Marshall, it is settled then. The bargain is made and cannot be broken as the master has said!" Rockford spoke in a quiet, yet triumphant tone. "You shall get your instructions..." suddenly the strange butler stopped speaking and slowly began turning his head around and up. Up to Avery Torrance's bedroom window. The unnerved chauffeur quickly moved back against the wall, his heart pounding in his chest by what he had just witnessed. Two sets of red glowing eyes staring directly up at him. Those of Clarence Rockford and those of the invisible being. He knew whatever he had witnessed could not have been human, but whatever it was, William Marshall had just made a bargain with it.

On wobbly legs, Avery made his way back to his bed and nervously sat down, sweat trickling off his face. Had those evil beings seen him watching in the dark? How could they have known he was there watching in the first place.

"Dear Lord, I pray that those evil things that looked up at my window only heard something outside the house and grew jumpy. A tree limb blowing against the window seal, the wind whistling through the shutters, just not me!" Crawling under the covers, Avery squeezed his eyes shut, trying to block out the horrible thing he had witnessed. His eyes flew open with the reality of seeing those eyes staring directly into his. "But...if they did see me...what would they do?"

CHAPTER 3

December 23, 1814

William Marshall was waiting below at the servant's back stairs when Avery Torrance walked down, feeling a little better since the first rays of sun had begun to rise. Knowing he always took his employer down to his office in town around 8:00a.m., the driver assumed Rockford had informed Mr. Marshall about the chauffeur's ease dropping on their late-night meeting. Out of respect, Mr. Torrance quickly fastened up his uniform coat.

"Good morning, sir. Did I fail to get word of an earlier departure this morning?" Pulling his pocket watch out, he noticed it was only 6:00a.m. Torrance glance up to see the owner of Marshall Mills watching him closely. "Have I done anything to displease you, Mr. Marshall?"

"Relax Torrance, I am very pleased with your service. I decided to drive myself to town this morning at the last moment, so I have been waiting down here to ask you to hook up the small carriage for me, nothing more." Still wearing his robe, William Marshall patted the carriage driver on the back. "I noticed Mr. Rockford was already having his breakfast so I opt out of asking him to speak to you and decided to wait and tell you myself."

"Then you will be needing the carriage ready by your usual time sir, 8:00?" Avery felt relieved that Mr. Marshall seemed unaware of his watching them the previous night so he followed behind him toward the kitchen. "I will grab a cup of coffee and get right on the hook up, Mr. Marshall."

"You may have some breakfast first if you like, Avery. I still have to get dressed and have my own breakfast before leaving." William stopped at the wide front steps. "One more favor Avery. I want you to bring my daughter down to the office around 10:00a.m. to spend some time with me. I will be bringing her home when I am finished for the day."

"I am certain Miss Pattie will enjoy some time with her busy father." Avery felt somewhat relieved seeing Mr. Marshall acting more like his old self. Maybe he had just had a very realistic nightmare during the night after hearing the conversation between his employer and the butler in the hallway. "Enjoy you day sir. I will be waiting at the entrance with the small carriage."

Always the reliable chauffeur, Avery Torrance had the smaller carriage hooked up with one white horse and waiting at the grand entrance by eight o'clock. After seeing Mr. Marshall off, the driver went inside to have a late breakfast, choosing not to eat earlier with the butler.

Avery was just finishing up his breakfast when Joyce Ann asked him to bring the carriage around for Pattie and her friend, Hattie. He stood waiting when the girls stepped out of the big mansion, Pattie in her rich red wool coat and matching hat and Hattie in her faded old grey wool coat, two sizes too big. As always, the cheerful driver greeted them both politely and helped them up on the high carriage then covered them with what he called a Christmas blanket. The red, green and white squares made it very seasonable and the sound from the sleigh bells ringing gracefully from the horse's reins as they pranced down the driveway, made for a magical ride for his young passengers. Avery chuckled from their giggles when the first flakes of snow began to fall then the sound of their young clear voices singing carols all the way to Sleepy Creek.

When they reached town, the streets were bustling with festival visitors and locals, filling the sidewalks and overflowing into the street. Mr. Torrance slowed the horses down and seeing no way safely through the crowd with such a big carriage and four horses, pulled the carriage over and stopped. After sizing up the situation, the patient driver turned around to face the girls.

"Kids, we have only made one block through this crowd and it's not safe to keep moving with all these people. I will

15

start looking for Mr. Clemons, the town constable and have him move these people out of the streets." His eyes scanned the crowd for any sight of the policeman as he continued speaking to the girls. "I cannot leave this carriage and go look for him. Someone or a loud sound could spook the horses and people could get hurt."

"We could walk to Mr. Marshall's office, Mr. Torrance." Hattie spoke up, seeing the bad situation and not wanting her friend up front to get into trouble with his boss. "It's not that far and I think Pattie needs to be there by ten."

Pattie smiled over at her friend and threw the blanket off, glad for the slow down and a chance to talk more alone with Hattie. She had been feeling nervous about visiting her father without her mother along, as it was on previous visits. "I agree with Hattie, Avery. Not only will we get to the office on time, but it will give Hattie and I a chance to talk some more on the way down." She gave the driver a reassuring smile when she noticed his concern face. "Avery, we will be perfectly safe among all these Christmas people. You needn't worry about us."

Seeing no other alterative after checking his pocket watch, he agreed. "Very well little ladies. Just be sure to stay on the sidewalk and watch out for carriages." Avery got down and helped the girls off. "You only have fifteen minutes to walk down to your father's office, so, no goofing off."

"Don't worry Avery, it's all downhill from here." Hattie gave him a big smile and the girls started walking toward the rock office.

Avery climbed back up to gather the reins in his strong grip as he looked around for Mr. Clemons. As he had done many times before, the carriage driver started speaking to his horses, who always seem to understand his words. "Fellows, as soon as that constable shows up and moves these people out of our way, we can move on down the hill too."

After waiting thirty minutes, Avery saw Mr. Clemons step from the small café across the street, wiping off his chin.

Immediately he spotted William Marshall's carriage sitting by the curb and panic sent him racing in the street blowing his whistle loudly. "Everyone, out of the streets! Please stay on the sidewalks and walk across where marked!" He raced over to the carriage, completely out of breath. "Please except my apology, Mr. Torrance. When I went in for a quick bite, these streets were empty, I swear." Noticing a heavy-set woman stepping into the street, the constable turned and blasted down on his whistle. "Madam, you cannot block traffic! For your own safety, stay on the sidewalks and follow the crossing signs!"

Avery was chuckling to himself as he watched the woman throw up her head in defiance and storm down the street grumbling to herself. He was so busy watching the people scurrying like scared rabbits he had not noticed Clarence Rockford stepping up next to the carriage. The driver was startled by the sound of his sudden voice.

"Mr. Torrance, pray tell, why are you sitting up here by the curb observing the shoppers instead of waiting in front of Mr. Marshall's office?"

"It would appear the streets have been blocked for over fifty minutes, Mr. Rockford, so our fine constable could grab a quick bite! Only now has this street been made safe to drive these four horses and large carriage down that hill without running over a large crowd of shoppers!" Avery stared down at his unwanted intruder. "I could ask you how you managed to get downtown yourself, Mr. Rockford, since I am driving the big carriage and Mr. Marshall left in the small carriage this morning while you were still having coffee after your very long breakfast."

"Frankly, I cannot see how that is any of your business, Torrance!" The stiff butler sneered. "If you must know, since it is obvious you have got poor eyesight, I rode into town this morning with Mr. Marshall and have been running errands all morning for him in town!"

"Listen Rockford, I personally saw Mr. Marshall off this

morning and I know without a doubt that he left alone!" Avery stared down into the butler's cold eyes. "I do not know what kind of fool you take me for, but I can swear I saw William Marshall come from the mansion by himself, climb up on the carriage, where I handed him his briefcase, then after bidding one another farewell, he drove away, while you were inside having coffee!"

The butler gave him an eyrie smile. "So, you did not see me climb up next to Mr. Marshall? Didn't you? I can assure you, I was seated in the carriage next to him, holding that brief case you handed me."

"Then if you were seated beside of Mr. Marshall in that carriage as you claim, you had to be invisible!" Avery was getting unnerved by this man's demeaner. "Jest all you like Rockford! I know what I saw. You did not come out with that dear man and when he left, he was alone!"

"Baa! You need some specs Torrance. Just ask Mr. Marshall if I rode in with him?" the butler laughed and waved his hand, filled with a stack of mail. "I am off to mail these. Is there anything you want me to mail for you?" he stared up at the carriage driver's vest pocket where he always kept his letters.

"When my letter is finished and I have completed the Christmas card to Charlotte, I can assure you sir, I will mail them myself." There was something creepy about the man staring up coldly with a menacing smile falling slowly over his face and Avery Torrance would not rest until he found out just what this man was up to. "The street is clear now Rockford, so I am going on down to Mr. Marshall's office and wait for his orders." Mr. Torrance took up the rein and looked down when the irate butler walked in close to the back horse and took hold of his bridle. "What now Rockford? You said I should be down in front of Mr. Marshall's office!"

"That's right Torrance and Mr. Marshall's other orders are for you to go straight inside the office and wait by the front door for Miss Russel!" This time there was no smile, just a smirk. "You are to take her by the mansion for her pitiful things and take the poor rag-a-muffin straight home! Miss Marshall will be returning with her father this evening, as you were told."

"Yes, that is what he told me early this morning while you were at the other end of the house feeding your face." The driver gave the butler a fake grin. "That leaves me with one question. How do you get back to the mansion Clarence? The small carriage has room only for two, unless our employer intends to change carriages with me so you can ride back with him. But that is very doubtful, since he has never driven the bigger carriage with four horses in front."

"There will be no switch, Mr. Torrance, there's really no need." The obnoxious butler merely stared. "I have my own means of travel. You best worry about getting your correspondence written and mailed off, while there is still time!" Letting go of the bridle, he laughed and walked away, leaving Avery wondering what he had meant by his last words: While there is still time.

CHAPTER 4

"Hattie, it was good to have you spend some time with my daughter." William Marshall had watched the Russel child take her final sip of the hot apple cider his secretary had waiting for the girls. Being a true southern gentleman, he helped her put her worn coat on and gave her a loving pat on the top of her dark locks. "I will be taking Pattie home later, so I have asked Mr. Torrance to take you by the house for your things and then take you home. Tell your family, the Marshall's wish them a Merry Christmas."

"Thank you, sir, I will and thank you for allowing me to come along with Pattie to pay you a visit in your office." Hattie gave Pattie one last hug, then tied on her scarf as William led her to the door.

Avery had watched his loving employer gently take the young girl's hand and walk her over to him where he waited patiently at the door. Mr. Torrance could see the concern written in the Russel child's eyes as the owner of Marshall Mills walked back over to his daughter and took a seat, pulling her in his lap. The kind chauffeur gathered Hattie's hand and led her out to the big carriage.

"How was your visit with Mr. Marshall this morning Miss Hattie?" Avery smiled down at the girl sitting next to him, looking back down the street where she left her friend.

Hattie turned around and sighed. "Mr. Marshall seemed to be in a merrier spirit this morning, Mr. Torrance. When Pattie and I arrived, we were surprised to hear him singing a carol, Hark the Herald Angels Sing. He was more talkative than he was last night and even laughed when I told him about our old mule, Jake, getting in the hog pen and getting chased by all four pigs." She giggled recalling the funny sight.

The driver noticed Hattie grow quiet as her face grew

thoughtful, as if something was weighing on her mind. "You know what I wish for this Christmas, Mr. Torrance?"

"Tell me sweet girl, what is in that pretty head of yours?" Avery started to wonder if this young girl had picked up the strange going on, inside that big mansion.

"I would feel a whole lot better if my friend Pattie could come to my house this year for the entire Christmas season!" Hattie stared straight ahead, her attention on the big mansion looming up in front of them.

"Now that is a big wish young lady. To get Pattie away from her parents during the holidays might prove an impossible task even for Santa Clause." As they started up the long drive to the mansion, Avery pulled the horses down to a slow trot to give them a few more minutes before she had to go inside for her bag. "Hattie, that is a most unusual request, even for the best of friends. Can you tell me why you want Pattie out of this house?"

Hattie turned to gaze up into the driver's gentle face and seeing genuine concern in his eyes wondered if he were aware of Pattie being afraid of her father's strange behavior. "My reason for wanting her to come live with me is not a selfish one, to have her all to myself, I grant you, sir! I am afraid for Pattie, Mr. Torrance, but I cannot tell you why. I made a promise to my dearest friend to keep her secret and I will never betray a trust."

"There's no need to tell me Hattie, I think I already know why that sweet girl is afraid." Avery knew he had Hattie Russel's attention when he pulled the carriage to a stop in front of the main entrance. "We will continue our conversation when we are back on the road. You and Pattie are not alone in this. You have an alley."

The driver and his rider looked up when the front door swung open and Pattie's personal maid came out carrying Hattie's cloth bag. "There's no need to get off the carriage sweet girl, I have packed your things for you at Mrs. Marshall's request, along with a note to your mother for allowing you to come at such a short noticed." Joyce Ann handed the bag to Mr. Torrance who had climbed off to place it in the back compartment.

"You did pack my diary, didn't you?" Hattie had turned around in the seat to watch the carriage driver secure her bag. "I will have lots to write in it tonight."

"You will find your lovely diary right on top, Miss Hattie." The maid gave her a genuine smile. "It was a delight to have you stay over. I could tell Miss Pattie enjoyed your visit very much."

"I had a wonderful time, Joyce Ann and hope Pattie can have a stay over at my home soon." Hattie returned the sweet woman's smile. "It's not as big or elegant, but it is warm, inviting, and filled with love."

"And it sounds perfect. Have a Blessed Christmas Hattie." Joyce noticed Avery walking back around to the driver's side and she raced around the back of the carriage to speak to him. "Avery, I hope I did not rush you, but Mr. Rockford told me to wait by the door with Hattie's things at 11:30 sharp!" she made a face. "How he knew the exact time has me dumb founded."

"Mr. Rockford informed you to wait? When, this morning before he left for Sleepy Creek?" Avery looked at her confused, knowing he had spoken to the butler about an hour ago.

"Left for Sleepy Creek? Avery are you alright? Clarence Rockford has been here all morning giving orders to everyone, including Mrs. Marshall!" the maid stared up at the house. "He suggested she have me pack that sweet girl's bag and have it ready when you arrived with her." Joyce leaned in close to him so Hattie couldn't hear her next comment. "The rude man insinuated poor children often have lice and spread it to those more fortunate than they are. If I would have been braver, I would have gladly slapped his sneering face!" the maid noticed Mr. Torrance hadn't taken his eyes off the house. "Avery, have you heard anything I have said?"

"I heard everything, Joyce Ann! I do not know what kind of man that is living inside a butler's uniform, but he is not only rude, he is unnatural." Avery felt a chill run down his spine knowing there was no way an ordinary human could be in two places at the same time. "Are you absolutely certain Clarence Rockford has been here all day, Joyce Ann?"

"He did go out around 9:30 to chop some firewood from the woodshed." Joyce watched the usual calm driver tremble. "Avery, why are you asking all these questions about Rockford?"

"Because, I saw him down town around 9:45, that's why. He could not have walked to Sleepy Creek in fifteen minutes." Something caught the driver's eye in the big hall window. Mr. Rockford was staring out at them. "Don't look now Joyce Ann, but we are being watched from the window in the entrance hall."

"Rockford?" the maid swallowed when Avery nodded his head. "That is creepy. Avery, there is no way you could have seen Rockford in town. He returned with the firewood at 9:45. Maybe you saw someone who resembled him walking down the busy street. I feel for the poor soul who did."

"Joyce Ann, I was waiting on the carriage for the streets to be cleared of festival shoppers when Rockford appeared and started speaking to me in his arrogant manner. So, unless he has a twin pretending to be him, it was defiantly the butler!" Catching movement on the passenger side of the carriage, Avery saw the shifty butler looking up at Hattie Russel. He moved swiftly to the driver's side and climb up speaking out to the confused maid who had not noticed the unwanted company. "Thank you, Joyce Ann. I will be sure to tell Hattie's parents what a polite, sweet and charming daughter they have."

Seeing the butler herself, Joyce Ann walked back around, moving in front of Clarence Rockford. "Your bag is all secure Hattie. I hope to see you again real soon. Young people have a way of brightening up a home." The maid forced a smile up for the butler. "Wouldn't you agree, Mr. Rockford?"

"I am sure you enjoyed being a special guest, young lady." The butler arched his brow.

"Please thank Pattie's parents for me Mr. Rockford and tell Mrs. Folly I especially liked my breakfast this morning. I really enjoyed that French bread with butter and jelly! It was yummy!"

"Yummy? Yes, of course, I shall deliver your charming message." He forced a smile. "I suppose a little farm girl like you must have felt like a real princess." Rockford's eyes fell over on the chauffeur who was watching the butler's arrogant behavior with discuss.

"Mr. Torrance, did you see anyone you knew on your way through town this morning?" A smirk fell on the butler's knowing lips.

"I did get a glimpse of the 'devil' among the street shoppers, Mr. Rockford!" Avery heard the maid try to smother her laughter as she raced back to the mansion. The chauffeur did not waver his stare on the hateful man. "If you will excuse us, Mr. Rockford, I will be taking our very charming guest home now." The driver gathered the reins and the horses responded in swift movements as the startled butler jumped to one side, making room for the big carriage to move pass him.

CHAPTER 5

Hattie Russel sat quietly, politely listening to the kind Chauffeur speaking nice words about the families that lived along the country road. "I have worked for William Marshall long enough to learn every person living on this beautiful old country road. I have never met a kinder, more generous bunch of people in my life, including your family." He glanced over and gave her a friendly wink. "Like the folks who live in that small white house there. The Baxter's gave me a whole ham just because I stopped to help Floyd fix the wheel for his wagon and help put it back on." He drove the horses a short distance and the Evan's farm came into view. "Now, Howard and Sarah Evans needed a ride to town to pick up their new wagon, so I gladly gave them a ride, hooked their new travel wagon up to the Carriage and brought them home. I told them I was happy to help a neighbor and never expected anything in return but that darling couple would not hear of it. I left with a brand-new shirt Sarah had made two sizes too small for her big husband!" Avery chuckled

"Have you met our nearest neighbors, the Morgan's? "Hattie saw the three Morgan children out in their big yard chasing their dog, before spotting the big carriage. All three waved and greeted the carriage driver and Hattie. Both riders return the wave as Hattie laughed. "I see you have met them."

"I had the pleasure of watching Billy, Bobby, and Bonnie last summer when all three kids had a slight fever and Milly and Marvin had to gather their vegetables so Marvin could take them to the market."

"What did they give you, Mr. Torrance?" Hattie was anxious to continue their previous conversation and wanted to hurry the story along.

"I ask for nothing and I still received a delicious apple pie as a reward." He smiled as the carriage left the Morgan farm behind them.

"Mr. Torrance, you are a good man to have around." Hattie knew he was avoiding their previous conversation and Russel farm wasn't much further. "Mr. Torrance, you said you think you know why Pattie is afraid and we would talk about it on the way to my house." Hattie turned in the seat to face him. "We are almost home sir, so maybe you need to tell me what you know."

"Hattie, I think Miss Pattie is afraid of her father. I saw a strange meeting in the rose garden below my window at exactly twelve o'clock, December 22." Avery notice Hattie was watching him tensely. "Mr. Marshall was having a conversation with some unseen being before Clarence Rockford, the butler appeared and began speaking."

Hattie relaxed, feeling relieved that someone else had witness the same kind of strange twelve o'clock meeting in the garden. "Could you hear anything they said to one another?"

"Bits and pieces. Something about having made a bargain with the invisible thing." Avery glanced over at Hattie when she gave a gasp. "I did hear a conversation in the central hallway between Mr. Marshall and Mr. Rockford. The butler same as ordered William Marshall to be at that meeting because he had made a bargain with 'him' meaning something powerful, because once made it could not be broken."

"Avery, you were right about Pattie being afraid of her daddy." Hattie grabbed his sleeve. "Pattie witnessed the same kind of meeting in the rose garden at twelve midnight. She said her daddy was talking to something invisible! What could this invisible thing be Avery? Surely not some ghost! The mansion is practically new so there is no way it can be haunted."

"I do not wish to frighten you Hattie, but I believe William Marshall was conversing with some kind of demon or the devil himself!" Avery Torrance knew he could trust Hattie Russel with his secret witnessing and he also felt he needed to tell someone not connected to the Marshall mansion what he knew in case something unforeseen happened to him.

"Avery, I feel there is something you're trying to tell me and I promise I will never share the things you are saying to me unless you find yourself in some kind of danger, my dear friend." The driver thought, such a small child with such a grown-up understanding mind. "Avery, why do think Pattie's daddy was talking to something evil?"

"From the red eyes staring up at me." Avery swallowed, still recalling the sudden fear that gripped him knowing he was well hidden in the dark window, not making a sound, but somehow, they had felt his presents.

"That thing saw you looking at him?" Hattie felt real fear and concern for Mr. Torrance. "I know you were careful not to be seen by your employer, so how did that thing know you were looking?"

"Not just the invisible thing, but also that butler, Hattie. Rockford was speaking and suddenly stopped, slowly turning his head around and up. Straight up at my window, both staring with glowing red eyes!" Avery had slowed the horses down as he recalled the terrible night. "No human could have seen me, standing back in the dark, but they did. Somehow, they had felt me watching."

"Golly gee Avery, that is horrible! Suppose they saw Pattie watching but never let on for some reason! If they felt you watching, surely they would sense her as well!" Hattie reached for his spare hand. "After that meeting, they did not appear in your room, did they?"

"Not that I could see, but I never got back to sleep, thinking they may come after me in the dark." Avery had hoped he had not frightened his sweet friend by telling her about his frightful experience. "Around one a.m. I thought I heard something moving outside my door but the crack under my door remained dark. Mr. Rockford seems to be testing me now. My question is, how can a person be in two different places at the same time?"

"Who, Mr. Rockford?" Hattie knew she would be home

soon after the driver turned the horses down her driveway.

"Rockford had been at the mansion all day, according to Joyce Ann, yet I had the misfortune of being confronted by him in town while I was waiting for the crowd to be moved!" Avery had slowed the horses to a slow walk to give them time to finish their conversation. "He lied about riding into Sleepy Creek with Mr. Marshall and said he had been doing errands all morning in town."

"Make that three places that creepy man was at the same time!" Hattie sat up excited over what she was about to revile. "Mr. Clarence Rockford was the one who greeted me and Pattie when we arrived at the office and he was there watching us the entire time. He excused himself right before you came inside!" Hattie noticed her mother waiting by the front door and knew she would be walking down to the carriage to get her and thank Mr. Torrance for bringing her home. She whispered to her friend when he pulled the horses up to a stop. "Please be careful Avery and watch after Pattie for me! Mr. Rockford cannot be human or else he is a great magician!"

"My guess would be a demon, since he had red eyes too." Avery Torrance climbed down to help his young friend off. "I will protect your friend Pattie with my life, Hattie Russel. Please do not worry, sweet girl."

"With your permission, I will write in my diary all you have told me Avery." Hattie noticed her mother walking toward them. "If the truth is written down and something happens, then the facts will be revealed and justice can be served!"

"Then by all means Hattie Russel, write down everything you know and the things that I have shared with you!"

CHAPTER 6

December 24, 1814

Avery Torrance had his breakfast very early to avoid the butler's arrival and was waiting by the small carriage for William Marshall to come out. Hearing the front door swing open, the devoted chauffeur stood straight as he watched the owner of the large estate walk out holding his daughter's hand. Waiting patiently, he listened to their conversation.

"I am very happy you loved your Christmas gifts, sweetheart. I hope you did not mind opening them before Christmas morning. I saw that beautiful Christmas dress in the showcase window two weeks ago and knew it was made for my Pattie."

"Daddy, it is the most beautiful Christmas dress I have ever received! Thank you, dear daddy." Pattie gave her father a tight hug. "That chest you gave me is very special too and I know just what I will use it for!"

"And what is that, my angel?" William caressed her blonde curls.

"All my special keepsakes daddy. Things I have collected over my life like my baby things, gifts from you and mama, special gifts Hattie made me over the years." Pattie watched him closely as she added. "Things I can take out and remember when I grow up and have children of my own to share my stories with."

Avery noticed Mr. Marshall trembled at her last words and realized his little girl had noticed his reaction as well. Her blue eyes fell on Mr. Torrance and he could read the fear in her young face as she asked

"Daddy, why must you drive into town again today. Why don't you let Avery take you to your office? You said you were coming back to spend Christmas Eve with me and mama this evening."

"And I will be precious, but your mama might need some last-minute Christmas items or something to attend to, so it is no problem for me to drive myself." William lifted his daughter up into his arms to give her an extra-long hug. "Now remember what I told you last night. Your very special Christmas present is waiting for you up in the attic and it is something that will be with you forever, but you must wait until tonight to open it darling before you get dressed for the Christmas Eve services. I've got to go now." He reached down and with trembling lips, kissed her forehead before climbing up on the small carriage and driving away.

Avery Torrance had watched the carriage go out of sight before turning around, thinking the sad girl had went back to the house only to notice her standing directly behind him, looking up with big serious eyes.

"Avery, would you please take me to the Russel Farm this morning. Mama is busy doing last minute things and cannot possibly get away but it is imperative that I pay my friend Hattie a visit this morning!"

"Miss Pattie, I do not mind taking you anywhere your heart desires to go but I must get your mother's approval first." Avery looked thoughtful, seeing her anxious face and knowing firsthand what it felt like. "You have already given your friend a lovely gift Pattie and I am certain you will see one another tonight at church."

"Please Avery! Please!" Pattie could not control the tears that laced her blue eyes. "I have to give Hattie another present and it cannot wait for tonight! I must take it to her this morning before…before I run out of time!"

At those words, Avery's bad feelings grew stronger as he managed to ask. "I do not know what you mean by running out of time, Pattie.

"It's just that Christmas is tomorrow and I just want her to have her present in time for Christmas morning, that's all." Pattie managed a weak smile before turning toward the house calling over her shoulder. "If you can get the carriage hooked up Avery, I will run in and get that present!"

As Avery Torrance was hooking up the horses in the carriage house, Clarence Rockford strolled inside. "I see you are getting ready to take the carriage out Torrance."

"That's right, Mr. Rockford. Was there something you needed from me?" Avery continued getting the carriage ready as he watched the butler move slowly around the large carriage house.

"Tell me, Mr. Torrance, did you sleep well night before last." The butler casually picked up a horseshoe and ran it around in his hands.

"I slept like a baby, Clarence, same as every night." His eyes caught the butler's "Why did you ask? I am certain you could care less if I get a good night sleep or not."

"I could swear you were up moving around in your room at midnight, on the stroke of a new day!" The irritating man open his palm to let the horseshoe fall hard on the stone floor causing the horses to get jittery.

"I assure you Rockford, if you heard something it was not me moving around at such an ungodly hour." Taking the reins, the carriage driver led the horses outside before the butler spooked them again in such tight quarters. "If you must know, I go up to my room every night exactly at eight and read by candlelight for one hour, then blow the candle out, crawl under my warm covers and go to sleep at nine." Avery looked the man over to find the hands of someone who had not ever done a day's hard work in his life. "Unlike some people who have life easy, I work hard from sun-up to sun-down and sleep comes easy to anyone who works hard for a living, Rockford!"

"Perhaps you walk in your sleep Torrance and do not realize you are walking around at midnight." His tone took on a menacing sound. "That could prove fatal Mr. Torrance, to a man who lives on the top floor and has a window looking down at the rose garden. To fall out on the earth would be bad enough but for you, poor fellow, there are pavers right below your window."

31

"Again Rockford, I do not get up once I go to bed and as far as the rose garden goes, I do not waste time gazing down at it in the winter months when there are no roses blooming so I keep my shutters closed except for one small opening to let fresh air in my room while I am sleeping!" Avery continued to walk the horses to the main entrance to avoid direct eye contact with the evil butler.

Rockford stepped in front of him, getting eye contact at last. "Yes, death can come to other things besides Roses this time of year, Avery Torrance. A word of advice! Mind your own business and stop asking so many questions! We would not want the next letter your poor wife receives be one telling her about her husband's unfortunate accident from sleep walking and falling from his bedroom window." The butler sneered and walked away leaving the chauffeur doubtful he would live until Christmas.

As his heart raced, Avery knew he must get his wife's letter in the postal that day before it closed early for Christmas Eve. He had written Charlotte about everything that had happened in the last few days concerning his suspicions on Clarence Rockford, Mr. Marshall and whatever that thing was in the garden that did see him watching. He had informed her about the butler being in three places at the same time and telling Hattie Russel, Pattie's best friend everything so she could write it in her diary. But Avery also knew, somehow, someway, he had to get the letter mailed without Rockford finding out by his evil means.

Lucas Peppers helped Pattie by carrying out the big heavy present to Hattie Russel, wrapped in the same Christmas paper as the first present. Avery helped his friend place the large gift on the storage rack at the rear of the big carriage before helping his serious passenger up to her seat. Before Avery could walk around to his side, his friend stopped him.

"Avery, a word my friend. Is there anything bothering you? You don't seem to be as happy as you were a few days ago when you got news that your cottage was almost completed and you might be able to send for Charlotte and the kids sooner than expected."

"I guess I'm just fretting because I haven't had the time to finish getting Charlotte's Christmas card filled out yet, not to mention needing to get this letter for her off today before the postal closes for the Christmas Holidays." Reaching into his vest pocket, Avery pulled out the envelope, addressed and stamped. Being a thoughtful friend, Avery did not want his best friend to know the real reason he was so upset for fear Lucas's life could be put in danger as well.

"Is that all." Lucas Peppers took the envelope from his friend's trembling fingers and placed it in a large bag over his shoulder. "I was getting ready to deliver Mrs. Marshall's Christmas mail along with my own and the staffs when Miss Pattie needed my assistance to help her carry that large gift out. It pays to have your own horse for times such as these. I will be more than happy to mail your letter Avery."

"That takes a load off of me my friend, thank you." Avery glanced up to see Pattie moving nervously in her seat. "I best be going. My young rider looks anxious about visiting her friend. I will try to finish Charlotte's Christmas card and get it off before the postal closes today. She won't get it in time for Christmas tomorrow but at least it will be postmarked Christmas Eve, 1814.

"Then good luck friend! You are welcome to take my horse when I return." The gardener climbed up in the saddle "See you later."

"Stay safe Lucas." Avery watched his friend ride away, with a strange feeling it would be the last time he saw him.

CHAPTER 7

Getting Hattie Russel's heavy gift from the carriage after helping Pattie Marshall down, Avery Torrance carried it over to the waiting girls. Hattie looked down at the large gift wrapped in the same beautiful Christmas paper adorning two big bows.

"Pattie, another gift for me?" The friends had never exchanged more than one gift each for Christmas, so this second gift came as a surprise to the humble farm girl. "I really feel bad about not having your gift ready yet. It will be ready tomorrow for certain and I planned to give it to you at the Christmas service. If it is ready by this evening, I will bring it by your house tonight."

"It will be special no matter what it is Hattie. It will be from you." Pattie gave her friend a hug, then her eyes fell on the package. "Hattie, don't open this gift until Christmas morning. I want it to be a surprise."

"Avery, if you give me the package, I can take it inside, then the three of us can have some milk and cookies before you leave."

"Hattie, Avery and I must be getting back to the house, but thank you for asking us to join you." Pattie looked at the heavy gift then the driver. "Avery will carry your gift inside for you, dear friend. It is pretty heavy so you better let Mark carry it up to your room when we leave." As Avery Torrance carried the gift in and sat it on a hall chair before returning, Pattie wrapped her arms around her very best friend, giving her a long hug, as if she did not want to let go. Pulling away, Pattie looked down with sorrow and said softly. "Goodbye Hattie. Never forget how much I love you." Before she burst into tears, Pattie rushed over for Mr. Torrance to lift her up, only to be stopped by Hattie Russel.

The soft-spoken Carriage driver watched the incredible actions of ten-year-old Hattie Russel as she removed the cross neckless that had hung around the young girls neck ever since he had known her and draped it around Pattie's small neck.

"Pattie, my dearest friend, I know this is not silver or gold, nor was it of great cost, but the love it holds outweighs any precious metals known to man. This cross is made from the dogwood tree, same as the cross on Calvary. Wear it to announce you are a child of God! Wear it to announce you are a follower of Jesus our Savior! Wear it to announce your heart is filled with the Holy Spirit and it will keep you safe always!"

"Hattie, I cannot take your beautiful cross. I know how much it means to you, dear friend." Pattie Marshall's eyes had filled with tears, knowing Hattie's favorite grandmother had given her the cross before she died and the sentimental farm girl had never taken it off until this day.

The patient driver could see from the girl's tears and emotions, they had incredible love for each other. One, a sweet and brilliant young girl born into wealth, who had a heart of pure gold for a poor farm girl and one, a clever and unselfish caring young farm girl who had been brought up to look on a person's inside and found the perfect friend in Pattie Marshall, opposites yet inseparable. Avery knew Pattie's fears were as real as his own and he prayed that he could protect the beautiful young girl from whatever those demons or her father were up to.

After having an early lunch, Avery hid out inside his bedroom to finish filling out his wife's Christmas card. Looking down at the beautiful card Susanne Marshall had given him two nights ago, he had an uncanny feeling that his Charlotte may never see this perfect card, or their finished cottage, even her husband, himself. Avery shook off the dreary thoughts and placed the card inside the matching envelope, addressed it and pasted on the stamp before placing it inside his vest pocket. He looked up at his reflection in the faded mirror and hardly recognized the face staring back. The

35

constant worrying and gripping fear had made him appear
gaunt. Checking his pocket watch, Avery saw he only had two
hours to get to town and mail the card. Lucas had returned and
left his horse saddled for his friend to make his way faster to
the Sleepy Creek Postal clerk before closing time. His plans
were altered when he reached the stables. A nervous William
Marshall was waiting just inside the door pacing the stable
floor.

"Torrance, there you are! Mr. Peppers said you would be
coming in to borrow his horse. But, before you leave for town,
I need the big carriage hooked up and brought around to the
side entrance. I will be needing it this afternoon to return to
town for some unfinished business then get back in time to take
Susanne and Pattie to the church service tonight. I am giving
you the night off."

"Of course, Mr. Marshall." Avery noticed how the usually
calm man was sweating and could tell he was upset over
something. "Sir, wouldn't the smaller carriage be easier to
maneuver through the crowded streets for your meeting. I will
be happy to take you and your family to the service tonight sir.
I have no plans."

"NO MR. TORRANCE! I do not want the small carriage
hooked up and I am very capable of driving my family to the
church without your help! I managed on my own before I hired
you, so kindly do as I say or find yourself another job!" The
carriage driver had never seen his employer so angry or upset
with him. Avery dropped his head as he removed his hat.

"Begging your pardon sir, I never meant to upset you or
suggest you could not drive the larger carriage. I will hook up
the horses right away and have it at the side door, just as you
wanted." Before Avery could walk toward the tack and the
bridles his employer stopped him.

"Avery, I should not have sounded so harsh toward you.
Please except my apology." William Marshall looked
genuinely sorry for his outburst as he placed a hand on the
coachman's shoulder. "Avery, you are the best driver I have

ever had and I could never replace you. Your job is safe. I am just tense because Susanne is upset with me for having to return to the office after dinner. The meeting will be brief and I assured her I could return in plenty of time to take us to the Christmas Eve Service tonight. I never meant to make you feel I did not want you to drive us, I just wanted it to be a family outing, nothing more."

"I understand Mr. Marshall. I should not have questioned your orders for hooking up the large carriage." Avery smiled, feeling better after seeing the old William standing in front of him. "I guess we are all feeling tense with last minute things left undone."

"Like getting your wife's Christmas card to the postal clerk before he closes?" William Marshall once again felt apologetic "My timing was bad and I have held you up. I will make it up to you Avery. I know how much you miss your family."

"Thank you, sir, that means a lot to me. Avery went to prepare the big carriage for Mr. Marshall. The card would have to wait until the postal clerk reopened on December 26.

Christmas Eve, 5 p.m.

Avery Torrance had eaten his dinner around four so the staff could prepare the Marshall's their dinner.

It was still early and he didn't feel like reading so he remembered the carriage house could use a good sweeping out. Avery opened back the double doors and began sweeping, his thoughts turning to his family and wondering what they were doing at that moment. He knew Fannie was getting excited with the thought of Santa arriving in a few short hours. Oh, how he missed the children's excitement over the Christmas season and Charlotte, just to hold her in his arms again. His thoughts were interrupted when he heard the back door shut.

Avery walked over by the open door and looked out. He saw William Marshall sneaking from the house carrying two large pieces of luggage and hide them in the back of the carriage. He quickly returned to the house and returned with more luggage. Grabbing the Christmas blanket from the back seat, he covered up the pile of luggage before returning to the house.

Avery scratched his head in confusion as he whispered to himself. "Mr. Marshall, what are you up to?"

He started to step outside when he heard a noise behind him and twirled around to find three men standing in the shadows, their faces unseen. Then his heart began to race with fear when he heard the familiar voice of Clarence Rockford coming from the man in the middle.

"Mr. Torrance, didn't I warn you to mind your own business?"

Avery watched in horror as the three men moved slowly from the shadows toward him. He was shocked to see all three had the face of Clarence Rockford as they circled him, blocking any way out.

CHAPTER 8

Present Time
November 26, 2025

Dear Diary, I am writing this tonight feeling almost as stuffed as Grandma Nettie's Thanksgiving turkey I enjoyed almost five hours ago. William is putting little Mattie to bed and reading her a bedtime story. I think he loves the stories as much as his daughter, maybe more since she is so small.

It was wonderful to have all the family this year for Thanksgiving and it really felt like old times. Matthew got real cute when he recalled the gifts I gave them for Christmas when I was too young to make much money and ask if I were going to buy him something this year from the five and dime. Knowing William and I were billionaires made the other brothers laugh at his ridicules statement. They laughed even harder when I told Matthew he would be lucky to get one Hattie Pattie cookie this year. It felt like old times hearing my brothers planning who would be doing what in the winter games. Ever since the Russel's and Brower's made a truce and became friends, the games have been played fairly until last year when the Caswell's moved in with Harvey Caswell, a recent widower and the owner of Handyman Harvey's Hardware, things got ugly again.

Jack and Wanda Caswell moved into the big six room home on Holly Street where Harvey ran his successful hardware store for over fifty years along with his deceased wife Hilda. Not having any children of their own, the couple made extra income by opening up five of the bedrooms during the Christmas Festival in Sleepy Creek. Now that Mr. Harvey's nephew moved in with his wife and three grown sons, the festival lost the extra rooms so my darling William saw a need to build a grand hotel at the far end of Reindeer Lane and like all the other

Joan Byrd

buildings in our fair town, he had it built in the 1800's style. The big two-store hotel is painted white with a luxurious wrap around porch and the huge staff of workers dress in 1800's attire. My adorable husband wanted to name it Hattie's Grand Hotel but I insisted he name it William and Hattie's Grand 1800's Inn and he loved the ideal. So now besides the many bed and breakfasts, including the Marshall Mansion Bed and Breakfast happily ran by brother Andrew and Shannon, there's more than enough room for all the festival visitors to Sleepy Creek.

Old friend, it's always a busy time in Sleepy Creek this time of year, especially for the Russel family. Nettie's cookie factory has become even more popular, so mama and my brothers ship out just as many cookies as we sale right here during the festival. Daddy and grandpa Gideon have really enjoyed their new farm equipment, but I have taken noticed from time to time, they brought out their old truck or tractor to plow a field or take produce to town. And daddy still insist on taking the old wagon to the town square for the Christmas shoppers. Grandma is having the time of her life watching after our little Mattie and declares she is just like her mama.

Galloping glazers! I cannot believe it has been 11 years since I solved that scary mystery, fell in love at ten-years-old to a 240-year-old-William Marshall! I suppose one day I will tell my daughter how I met and fell in love with her loving daddy, or just let her read you, my beautiful old friend.

Lately I have been having strange dreams about walking through that old mansion before it became a lovely bed and breakfast and in the dream, I am still 10 years-old. I keep searching for something and I end up on the top floor, all alone. This thing I am looking for draws me to the West wing to a small room overlooking the rose garden. I have the strangest feeling I'm not alone in the room and then I hear what sounds like a grandfather clock striking twelve somewhere below me, then the sound of a bed cricking, then footsteps walking slowly to the window overlooking the rose garden. When the shutter

40

moves back and the window slowly opens, I snap awake, my heart pounding. It's not because I am afraid of the lovely old mansion since I got that box from the attic and the Lord sent the horrible demon back to his master, that makes me apprehensive. It is the present mystery of what's going on in that mansion now. The guest staying in the west wing have been frightened from strange sounds at midnight. My brother and his wife Shannon have not heard any sounds yet but Andrew said when the room became vacant, he would stay up until midnight to hear for himself the sounds. There have been reports of unusual sounds also in the library, late afternoon, so William has agreed to go with me on Saturday to check the west wing and see if he can recall how the house was laid out before the big renovation transformed his mansion into a bed and breakfast. Up until now, my poor darling could not bring himself to go back inside his old home in fear of remembering what he had done to his first family and loyal staff back in 1814.

Now, because of the dream leading me to the west wing and the reported sounds coming from the same spot and at the exact hour, I cannot help the nagging feeling that I left something or worse still, someone, undiscovered in that old mansion 11 years ago. Who could I be forgetting? Aunt Hattie's dairy gave the names of those missing, Susanne, Pattie and the staff, so who was left behind. I saw all their spirits come out and leave with our Lord. Surely Jesus would have known if someone were still trapped inside. My thoughts then were filled with so many emotions. Getting that thing out of the attic, then down to William before I got trapped inside myself. Actually, seeing and speaking to the ones Aunt Pattie had written about and the sadness I felt knowing William would be leaving me forever and I would never see him again. But God had a plan for me and William and when I became 20, the miracle accrued that brought him back to me.

Now I am 21 years-old and my William is 31, another God-given gift when he returned from heaven at 30. We were married last Christmas day and almost nine months later our baby girl was born on September 1 and at four months old, she is defiantly a daddy's girl.

The other good thing that happened when William returned was to take over his role as president of the company and let me open my own detective business. When the small business closed next to the cottage, William insisted I make it my office to be near him, so I hung my shingle, The Missing Piece Detective Agency, over the front door and got my first case almost instantly. With my good friend Jane Tanner working as my secretary and Matthew, my boy Friday, who proved to be good at helping find clues from old records, we had already solved ten mysteries and are happily finishing up the last one until after the new year. The team had worked hard and deserved time off for all the busy festival activities.

Dear diary, I hear William coming up so I must close now to give the love of my life my full attention. Hattie Russel Marshall.

CHAPTER 9

Hattie had just wrapped up her latest case and was busy filing away the McCoy case in her old antique file cabinet. Keeping her records on paper seem to suit her office and practice, living in Sleepy Creek dating back to the 1800's. Her thoughts turned to her devoted husband who had lovely walked her to the office before taking their daughter to the farm then made his way to the old mill. How romantic William had been the previous night when he entered the bedroom with a bottle of champagne, two glasses and chocolate covered strawberries. Hattie could still feel his warm lips on hers as they made love until the wee hours of the morning. Her beautiful thoughts were interrupted when a light knock came on the old chestnut door and Jane Tanner stuck her head inside.

"I know you had planned to close the office early today Hattie, but there were two very important calls after you came in and I thought you might be interested in both so I gave them an appointment this morning." Jane made an I'm-sorry face but Hattie just laughed. "So, my job is still safe, boss?"

"I could not possibly replace you, my friend, so who are these very interested clients?"

"Your brother Andrew said he could not wait another day to speak to you about the strange noises in the mansion." She glanced down at the second caller's name. "I gave this young woman the 10:00 appointment because there was something very haunting about her last name. Emily Charlotte Torrance. She says she came here from South Carolina to find out about her missing great-great-great grandfather. That's as much as she would give me on the telephone."

"Torrance?" Hattie walked over to the office window and pulled back the curtains to see the streets beginning to cover with a fresh blanket of snow. "Torrance." She repeated the familiar name. "I am certain I have heard that name somewhere before."

"Maybe Miss Torrance can shed some light on who he was and why his name is so familiar to us. She said her plane landed at the airport in Ashville and has rented a car to drive to Sleepy Creek." Jane checked her watch. "At 8:30, she said she was about one hour away from our town, so I gave her 10:00 and Andrew is coming any moment." Hattie's secretary could tell her smart detective friend's mind was already turning over thoughts in her bright head. "What have you come up with? I know when your detective juices are flowing."

"With Emily's grandfather being three greats back, he would have had to live in the 1800's!" Hattie's eyes lit up. "You don't suppose this Mr. Torrance had something to do with the mystery of the old mansion?" Both girls heard the bell over the office door ring, then the sound of Andrew's voice calling his sister's name. "Andrew, we are back in the office. Come on in." Seeing his handsome smile, Hattie walked over to hug her oldest brother.

"I thought you might be dropping by today after telling me yesterday you could use a good detective." Hattie motioned to the seat across from her desk before sitting down. "Let me guess, the guest on the west side have been disturbed by the unusual noises again."

"I am afraid it has gotten worst. The Claxton family have been reserving that suite every holiday since Shannon and I opened the inn and this morning they turned in their key. I luckily found them the last room at your hotel so they wouldn't have to go home and miss the rest of the festival." Andrew had a worried look cross his face. "The lovely couple really liked the suite because it overlooked the rose garden, decked out this time of year with our giant Christmas tree, arrayed in twinkling white lights and the life size reindeers grazing about the garden, all adorned with wreathes of holly and lighted to match the big tree." Andrew smiled up at his sister. "You always had an eye for the perfect holiday displays little sister and along with my artistic-talented wife, the garden is a hit every holiday." His face grew serious. "But this 'ghost' that keeps haunting the mansion is putting a damper on everyone's mood, especially Shannon's. If something isn't done to get rid of that intruder, my wife has threatened to take the children and go stay with her parents. So far, we have protected the children from knowing about the strange sounds, but it's just a matter of time before someone says something in front of them or they hear the noise for themselves."

"Have the sounds been heard in the library recently?" Hattie knew the only way for her to get close to uncovering this mystery was to spend the night in the old mansion herself.

"Is last night recent enough, Hattie?" Andrew closed his eyes as he recalled the unusual sounds he had witnessed for himself. "I decided to sit in the library at the same spot several, guest had reported the sound coming from. The first sound was like feminine footsteps walking into the library, pausing, then moving toward the old desk in the corner. A more-manly set of footsteps then followed the others. The sound of a drawer opening and a soft click, like someone opening a lock."

"So, you never saw the drawer actually open?" Hattie remembered seeing the shutter opening and the window rising, seemingly by itself in her recurring dream but maybe in real life it could never happened.

"No Hattie, the drawer remained closed. I just heard the strange sounds and had the unusual feeling I was not alone in that library." Andrew recalled the reason Bill and Caroline decided they could not stay in room 6 another night. "Before the Claxton's handed over their key apologetically, they reported the reason was the sounds had grown louder, starting with the old grandfather clock in the central hallway striking the midnight hour. The noises drove them to their feet so they walked over to where the sound was coming from and they could easily hear the shutter open briefly, then stop before the sound of the window opening. The tired couple said they gazed down into the garden expecting to see the big tree and reindeer aglow with lights but instead they swear they saw three men turn and look up at them with eyes as red as a Christmas bulb."

"Then what happened?" Jane had been listening, her eyes round as saucers.

"Caroline said they grabbed each other, squeezing their eyes shut. When they finally regained their nerves, they took a breath and peered back down and saw only the Christmas display." Andrew heaved a sigh. "That's when they decided to leave and not being able to get back to sleep, spent the remainder of the night packing."

"I remember room 6 well Andrew. The west end of the top floor was obviously the servant's quarters when William had the big mansion built in 1804. There were exactly nine rooms up there, some larger than others. When Daddy, Grandpa Gideon, and I went up on the hill to look around inside the mansion, we found everything in remarkable shape, despite it's age. It was so large, daddy suggested we split up to check it out and call out should one of us find something of interest. I found the second set of steps, tucked away on the far end of the center hallway. I gathered right away it must have been the servants due to the narrow and steeper risers and no candle sconces attached to the walls." Hattie paused and reached for her copy of The Box in the Attic. "It has dawned on me, if there were nine rooms on the west side, why were there only seven trapped spirits inside that old mansion? The butler, Mr. Rockford, would make eight, so who am I forgetting? It doesn't make any since."

Matthew Russel walked inside the office carrying a stack of mail and overheard Hattie's last comment. "Hey sis, maybe the answer can be found in Aunt Hattie's diary instead of your best-selling book!" he dropped the mail on her desk before slapping his brother playfully on the back. "Hi Andrew, what brings you to town this morning?"

"Business Matthew! I need to hire a good detective before I lose all my loyal guest and my beautiful family due to my haunted Bed and Breakfast!" Andrew remained serious as

Matthew pulled up a chair and reached across to pat his sister on the head.

"Then you came to the right place, big brother. Our Hattie is the best detective around and if there's one thing she knows, it's solving mysteries of the Marshall Mansion."

"And that is why I am here, 'little brother'!" Andrew turned to his sister. "Hattie, I know this is a busy time for William, but is there any way the two of you can move into the mansion during the festival? It would be the perfect time with room 6 available."

"Oh, the spooky haunted room!" Matthew pretended to shiver. "Maybe I should come along and protect you both."

"Matthew, run outside and be on the lookout for our next client!" Hattie noticed his unhappy face, thinking this would be the last workday until after the New Year. "You can relax, brother, I pretty much can handle this one on my own so you can just take the time to have a holly jolly bunch of fun." She glanced down at the girl's name. "Both cases are most likely connected anyway. Her name is Emily Torrance."

"Torrance?" Andrew and Matthew repeated the name in unison as Jane pulled Matthew up and over to the door.

"I will come with you Matthew and let Hattie and Andrew talk." Hattie's girlfriend looked back to give her a wink and the young detective waved gratefully and waited for the door to shut behind them.

"Andrew, you know I would be more than happy to stay at the mansion, but I'm not sure William is ready to sleep in there all night, even with adorable me by his side." Hattie relaxed when she watched her brother finally smile. "William hasn't been near his old home ever since he returned. There are far too many bad memories tied up inside that old place and we have limited any discussions concerning his once grand estate. William is completely content living in the rock cottage and it is where we grew to love one another eleven years ago." Hattie glance down at the picture of her husband displayed in an antique frame and could feel her heart flutter as it did every time she saw his handsome face. "I knew I had to tell William about the recurring noises in the mansion, because I needed his help in remembering the layout of its original plans. Especially the servant quarters in the west wing and who stayed in the one looking down at the rose garden."

"Did you make any changes in the library or is it pretty much the same as William and Susanne had it in the 1800's?" Andrew felt more at ease knowing his sister was on top of the case. "The high-back armchair I was sitting in was the main spot I felt a presence near me, almost beside me. Better still, under me. A weird sensation."

"I wouldn't know the feeling, Andrew. I have never had the pleasure of sitting on a ghost's lap before." Hattie laughed when Andrew sat up, eyes wide open in shock. "I will speak to William, Andrew. I realize the only way I can discover what is going on in that mansion is to stay there and sleep in room 6. If William cannot bring himself to sleep over in his old home, I will work something out so I can spend a good part of my day with William and Mattie. I am sure he will plan to work from home to be near me if he chooses not to sleep at the mansion."

"Thank you, sis! I wouldn't ask if I wasn't at the end of my rope!" Andrew felt tears forming in his eyes as the pressure was lifted from him. "I know Shannon will feel more at ease with you there working on the case."

"Please tell Shannon to stop worrying. I will get to the bottom of what is causing this disturbance and I will not rest until I find out the truth. The missing person should be revealed very soon and then the pieces of the puzzle will start to go together. Andrew, I will not let you down, I promise." Brother and sister got up to hug one another. "William has promised to come with me Saturday and help me remember how the mansion looked before it became a bed and breakfast. There is more to this mystery than just some poor forgotten ghost wondering the old mansion. The fact that no one can remember who the ninth servant was and what made everyone forget, past and present. The fact that Jesus did not call the ninth lost

48

servant's spirit out to take up to heaven. Why Aunt Hattie did not include in her diary the missing person with the staff trapped inside. What did the woman ghost take from the drawer and why did she open a secret compartment in her desk?"

"Wow, little sister! You are quite the detective!" Andrew shook his head in disbelief. "And I thought the case was only about our haunted bed and breakfast."

"Once I have the answer to all those questions, the puzzle will come together and the mystery will be revealed!" Hattie said, excitement showing on her beautiful face.

CHAPTER 10

"Thank you for seeing me, Mrs. Marshall." The petite blonde had been shown into the small office exactly at ten o'clock. She looked around at all the family portraits hanging on the wall. At the far end a large frame revealed one small girl surrounded by eight boys, different ages. "Is that you and your brothers who are in your book?"

"Yes, that would be the Russel children eleven years ago." Hattie got up to point out the group. "Andrew, Peter, Philip, James, John, Matthew, Simon, Thomas and me, Hattie at ten." Hattie smiled at the next portrait. "This one is of my grandpa Gideon, grandma Nettie, my mama, Carolyn, and my daddy, Adam."

"It's good to finally have a face to go with the characters." The shy girl blushed. "I mean, your family." Hearing Hattie chuckle she relaxed and pointed to the handsome couple in the middle frame. "That has to be you and your William. He is even better looking than I imagined when reading the book."

Hattie had noticed her new client had been clutching a very old box she had laid into her lap when she took a seat and her eyes fell on it the moment she said, "Your book changed my life, Mrs. Marshall."

Hattie smiled at Emily Torrance when she finally glanced up. "The mystery of the Marshall mansion has brought many comments my way, Miss Torrance, but your remark is very different. May I call you Emily? And I would like it if you called me Hattie."

"Yes, I would like that, Hattie. It did seem strange calling you Mrs. Marshall since we appear to be close in age." She finally smiled, making her even prettier. "Hattie, the reason I said your book changed my life is because of some old letters and Christmas cards I inherited when my granny Torrance passed away in the spring. They belonged to my great-great-great grandmother, Charlotte Torrance. After receiving the loving letters and cards, I read them repeatedly, especially the last letter grandfather sent Grandma Charlotte. Avery wrote a chilling letter describing many strange things going on at the Marshall Mansion."

Hattie sat straight up in her desk chair at the mention of Marshall Mansion and knew this Mr. Torrance had to be a part of the staff. Maybe he was the missing employer, the spirit haunting the big house. She prayed the letter was in the box Emily Torrance held so tightly. "Emily, did your grandfather Avery work for the Marshall's?"

The young women titled her head in confusion before lending forward. "You surely must know him, Hattie. My grandfather, Mr. Torrance was mentioned in both your book and your aunt's diary!"

Suddenly it all came back into her memory, like a window shade being raised to let the sunlight in. "Of course! Mr. Torrance, the Marshall's chauffeur!" Hattie jumped to the floor and began pacing the room. "How did William not see his carriage driver with the other spirits when they stepped outside after being trapped in the house for 200 years? Why did Pattie, Susanne, the cook, the twin maids, the three personal maids and the gardener, Mr. Peppers, not mention Mr. Torrance?" she stopped pacing long enough to look down at the startled girl. "The only one Aunt Hattie mention leaving the mansion was the butler, rotten old Mr. Johnson, alias Mr. Rockford!"

"Yes, Grandfather Avery mention Clarence Rockford in several letters." Emily shivered recalling the last letter. "In my grandfather's letters to his wife, he spoke of his best friend, Lucas Peppers, the gardener. I wonder why his best friend never mentioned grandfather?" Emily watched the young detective as she returned to pacing. "Hattie, what made a best friend forget his friend ever excised?"

"That's it!" Hattie slid back down on the chair and looked across the table when the lightbulb went off in her brilliant head. "You just hit on something Emily! Someone or some being caused not only Lucas Peppers to forget his friend Avery Torrance, but everyone living inside that mansion. And by no mention later in Aunt Hattie's diary, she too had also forgotten the gentle carriage driver. Somehow, the memory block carried over 200 years so everyone in Sleepy Creek, myself and William included, had our memories blocked by the same powerful being!" Hattie glanced down at her book as it dawned on her even the ones who read The Box in the Attic also had their memory blocked and no one remembered Mr. Torrance or why he was not mentioned after Pattie took the chest to her friend Hattie on Christmas Eve alone with the carriage driver. Hattie got back up and walked to the office window to find the snow still falling.

"What kind of power could perform this? I knew I was forgetting something and..." Again, Hattie stopped, remembering Andrew's encounter in the library, the footsteps walking to Susanne's desk, the sound of a drawer opening, a soft click, the sound of a key opening a secret door inside the old desk. As she often did, she began thinking out loud. "Avery had to get his stationary from someone in the mansion, most likely Susanne Marshall when she came into the library. If his ghost is roaming around the mansion's library and the top floor's west wing, why didn't the Lord call for him to come out? The other's may have been mysteriously blocked, but nothing could remove the Almighty's eternal memory!"

"Hattie, did you say my grandfather could be haunting the Marshall Mansion?" Emily's fingers moved nervously over the box. "Could that evil butler and other thing with red eyes my grandfather wrote about, put him in some hidden place in the mansion and...seal the poor man inside?" her emotions brought out uncertain tears, wondering what kind of agony her loving grandfather might have suffered, alone in some dark small space, knowing that he would surely die there, trapped inside.

"Emily, you had to read about the butler and the thing in the rose garden from your grandfather's letter. Did you bring your grandfather's letters and Christmas cards he sent Charlotte?" Hattie looked hopeful as the young woman sat the old box on the desk and opened the lid, reviling a stack of letters, tied together with a blue satin ribbon and three very old 1800's Christmas Cards, tucked carefully inside.

"I hope you can find some clues in these letters Hattie, but the last one he wrote, sends chills up my spine and puts fear in my heart for the dear man. I shudder to think what happened to him after he finally got to send his last correspondence to Grandmother Charlotte."

"I am certain I can find many clues in Mr. Torrance last letter to Charlotte. The puzzle has started to come together already. The first missing piece was discovering who Mr. Torrance was and the second piece of the puzzle is learning who is haunting the mansion and why his spirit was walking over to Susanne's desk in the library, to repeat the night he borrowed some stationary to write his letter to his wife. The poor lost spirit repeats the ritual again and again during the holiday festival." Hattie picked up the stack of letters and reached for the one on the bottom, dated December 23, 1814. Avery Torrance's very last letter to his wife Charlotte.

CHAPTER 11

December 23, 1814

"My dearest Charlotte, I write this letter with a tortured mind and a growing sadness in my inmost heart that I may never see you or our adorable children again. It's not my health that concerns me for I have never felt better a day in my life than I do at this moment. There are certain circumstances that have altered my entire life and the hope of escaping several unknown forces working around me, seem to be sweeping in to block any way out.

It's not just for myself I worry, but the sweet innocent Marshall child, who apparently feels the same evil forces closing in on everyone living within the big mansion, with a couple of exceptions, William Marshall, my once friendly and kind employer, and Mr. Clarence Rockford, the butler. Rockford appears to be the instigator behind whatever is going on.

It was little things at first that brought on my suspicions. Young Pattie Marshall's strange behavior towards her best friend, Hattie Russel. Making sure her friend got her first present early, unlike previous Christmas' when Pattie and Hattie exchanged their gift to one another at the church's sharing the gifts service on Christmas day. The sweet kid insisted her mother let her deliver the gift to the Russel's farm, out in the country. I watched as Hattie opened the gift. It was an expensive looking diary with her name written in gold letters across the top. I overheard the Marshall child ask her friend to record everything they did together, starting with the holidays. I believe Pattie's motive was for Hattie Russel to keep a record of everything in case something unforeseen happened to her.

When I was waiting in the library for Mrs. Marshall to

return after having her dinner, which was her habit every evening, so I could borrow this lovely stationary I am writing on, I overheard Mr. Rockford and Mr. Marshall having an argument in the hallway outside. The arrogant butler same as ordered Mr. Marshall to meet him in the rose garden at midnight.

I know my beloved wife must be wondering why I did not get my writing paper from Mr. Marshall instead of his thoughtful wife Susanne like I usually did. It was his reaction when I brought up the subject to borrow a few more sheets of stationary. The once polite and generous man yelled at me asking if I were not paid enough to buy my own stationary? I merely apologized, feeling like a fool for asking for what he had always given me since I started driving for the family, knowing I was saving most of my pay for you and the children. I remember his kind words to me when he offered to supply all my stationery and stamps, so I could write you often. He said, "Avery, I know you are a devoted family man and to take on this position as my chauffeur would mean being separated from Charlotte and your children. Writing can never replace being with loved ones in person, but it can help bridge the distance between you and them. Feel free to ask me whenever you need more stationery and stamps."

Charlotte, this is only one small change in Mr. Marshall. He has become moody, angry, quiet at other times and there are moments he appears to be extremely anxious and afraid over something.

The night I borrowed the stationary from Susanne Marshall, I also received the perfect Christmas card meant just for you, my darling Charlotte. This letter had to be written first to tell you all I know in case something happens to me. I will see that it gets mailed tomorrow because if my fears are real, my time may be running out. I do not wish to sound morbid my love, but after what accrued last night at midnight, things appear to have gotten worse. Mr. Marshall was down in the rose garden conversing with something invisible. At first, I assumed the confused man was speaking to God, because he was verbally conversing with a being. I could not make out his soft words from three floors up on the top floor. It did not take long to realize the invisible being was nothing like our blessed Lord. Clarence Rockford suddenly appeared from out of nowhere, as if by magic and begin his demanding words. I heard words like once a bargain has been made it cannot be altered. Before he could complete another sentence, he suddenly stopped speaking and slowly his head began to swivel around toward the house then up to the window where I was hiding. Charlotte, the freaky thing was how well I was hidden in the dark room, the shutters cracked barely open as was the open window. No ordinary person could have seen me up there but somehow, they did, Mr. Rockford and the invisible being. I realized the only way they could have known I was up on the top floor watching was their power to sense my presence. I swear I saw two sets of red eyes, glowing brightly, and staring directly into my eyes. I still shake reliving the nightmare.

My darling Charlotte, please do not think I am losing my mind or imagining these horrible things, but the next morning after the midnight meeting, that creepy butler appeared beside my carriage while I was in Sleepy Creek waiting for the streets to be cleared of people. I had just delivered Pattie Marshall and her friend Hattie Russel downtown to visit Mr. Marshall when the festival shoppers had the streets blocked for through traffic. The kids walked the short distance to the stone cottage office while I waited for safe passage. So naturally I was startled to hear the butler's voice next to the carriage. Only an hour earlier I heard the brass man shouting out orders to the staff, so I required as to how he got to town knowing Mr. Marshall had taken the smaller carriage out earlier that morning and I drove the large carriage. I know my good friend Lucas would never loan him his horse to ride to town. Rockford had the nerve to tell me he had ridden down with Mr. Marshall and had been running errands all morning for him. Then after I rebuked his statement, he sneered and said I needed some new spectacles and ordered me to get down to the office and take Miss Russel back to the mansion then home.

Then I found out later by Joyce Ann, you remember, Pattie's personal maid, that Clarence Rockford had been at the mansion the entire day giving orders. Then on the way to Russel farm, Hattie and I exchanged theories on what we knew and after telling her about Rockford being in two places at the exact same time, Hattie said, make that three places. The scary butler had been at Mr. Marshall's office when the girls arrived and he stayed until I drove up with the carriage.

Hattie has started a diary of all the strange things that have been going on with William Marshall. The sweet child is afraid for her friend Pattie and the brilliant young lady has picked up on the same things I have, so now I know there will be a witness to what has happened through the pages of the young girl's diary.

Charlotte, my beloved, the old clock in the central hallway has just struck twelve and four o'clock comes early. I strive to have my breakfast before Mr. Rockford shows his face in the servant's hall. Besides, I must get Mr. Marshall's carriage ready and waiting at the front entrance for his exit. I hope I am just imagining all these weird happenings and nothing comes of it. After all, it is a stressful and busy time for Mr. and Mrs. Marshall, as well as the staff. Please look for your special Christmas card soon. It's almost finished. I wish our Christmas could be spent together. I miss you all dreadfully. Never forget, Miracles appear on Christmas Eve and hope blooms in the spring. With deep devotion and love. Your Avery.

CHAPTER 12

After Hattie read Avery Torrance's intriguing letter out loud, Emily Torrance leaned forward, an anxious expression on her face. "Hattie, what do you think happened to grandfather? It has been 211 years since he vanished, not just in body, but oddly from everyone's minds. Those who lived in Sleepy Creek back in 1814 and even those living now. It's all so strange!"

"I'm afraid everything connected to the Marshall mystery has been strange, Emily. The fact that demons were involved make it complicated and different from other cases." Hattie stood back up and began pacing around the room, trying to sort out the many questions running through her pretty head. "Demons are angels, fallen angels, that fought on the side of Lucifer, the once beautiful angel of light, now the angel of darkness. God gave all the angels choice, same as he gave humans, but He also gave them special powers. Powers that humans do not possess." Hattie glanced out the window. "Just suppose angels have the power to block memories, so things we once knew was suddenly wiped from our mind." Hattie turned and smiled at her client, who watched and listened with fascination. "It is just a theory. I will go speak to my old friend, Reverend Westly. He preached one Sunday on the power of God's angels." She took her seat and picked up the letter.

"Your grandfather's suspicions toward Mr. Rockford, the butler, prove to be true. He described in the letter how the demons stopped their conversation with William and turned, his word was, swiveled their heads toward the house and up to the window to stare at him with red glowing eyes, just like the demon in the attic."

"It was obvious that evil butler started harassing Grandfather Avery after that incident." The petite granddaughter felt relieved that Hattie Russel was interested in her missing relative and her hopes for finding his body, what was left of it, could at last be discovered and properly buried. "Your Aunt Hattie mentioned Grandfather Avery a few times, then her focus turned to the disappearance of her friend Pattie and the other staff members trapped inside the big mansion."

"The fact that Aunt Hattie never recorded the conversation between herself and Avery, is one piece of the puzzle I must discover. I recall her writing about him saying nice things about all her neighbors, but the very thing she should have written was their serious talk." Hattie shook her head. "I am certain your grandfather had hopes that Hattie would write their words down in case something happened to him." She picked up the old diary she kept on her desk. "I have read this book all the way through, over and over, especially the Marshall mystery, and I can assure you, that conversation was omitted. The power that blocked everyone else, blocked my aunt's memory of their conversation or…" Hattie stared at the old book. "Or maybe Hattie did write it down and for some reason, the page went missing or…went blank." Hattie made herself a mental note to look up that date in Aunt Hattie's diary and see if she could lift up the missing words she knew were there somewhere. For now, she needed time to do some research and investigating and Emily Torrance needed a place to stay in a town filled to the brim with festival visitors.

"Emily, I will get right on this case and I know without asking if you have a place to stay while you are here in Sleepy Creek. This time of year, our old town is busting with festival visitors, mostly repeat customers who feel the true Christmas spirit. All the inns and William and Hattie 1800's Inn, our only big hotel, are booked, but the good Christian citizens in our close community take people in when all the rooms are full."

"I did notice the overflowing crowd of happy people mingling on Main Street when I drove in." The shy girl looked embarrassed as she glanced down. "My mind was preoccupied with my grandfather's disappearance. I never one time considered where I might find a room in your Christmas town with the festival in full swing. I could drive to the nearest town and find a room."

"Emily, that won't be necessary, besides, all our neighboring towns are most likely filled up by now due to Sleepy Creek Festival becoming even more popular ever since my book came out." Hattie chuckled "It appears all my readers want to see the Marshall Mansion for themselves. I know just the family who has a spare room waiting just for you. My old room at the Russel family farm." Hattie had been dialing her old home place while she talked and smiled as the familiar voice picked up the receiver.

"Hello grandma, can you make my new client a guest in my old room? Her name is Emily Torrance, from South Carolina. Matthew is available to show her the way out to the farm."

"Hattie darling, did you say Torrance? That name sounds so familiar." Nettie bounced Mattie on her knee and smiled at the baby's giggles. "Is she someone from Sleepy Creek High School?"

"Nowhere close, grandma. Emily is here to find her missing grandfather."

"Hattie dear, I don't recall anyone from Sleepy Creek reported missing. You know I watch the nightly news and read the local paper daily."

"I can assure you, my precious grandmother, you would not find Emily's grandfather on the news or in our local paper." Hattie knew her next statement would shock the dear, woman, whose mind was as sharp as it had always been. "The reason you cannot recall the name Torrance is because he has been blocked from your mind. And before you can object, my mind was also blocked until Emily showed up. He was part of the 200-year-old Marshall Mystery."

"Torrance?" Nettie studied the familiar name. "The man's name is right on the tip of my tongue. Part of the Marshall Mystery, so Aunt Hattie had to mention a Mr. Torrance."

"His full name was Avery Torrance and he was William's

Chauffeur, the carriage driver!" Hattie heard her grandmother gasp. "I know, it gave me a jolt too. The night I brought that box from the attic and the spirits were finally free from the trapped house, I was overwhelmed with emotions. Seeing Pattie and those trapped inside for 200 years, that horrible ugly demon who threatened William, being in the presence of Jesus, our Lord and the fact that I would be saying goodbye to the man I had given my heart to at ten-years-old made my thinking cloudy. It never occurred to me that Mr. Torrance was not among the spirits coming from the house."

"Everyone forgetting someone as important as the carriage driver had to take a powerful force." Nettie put little Mattie down in her playpen and gave her a playful pat on the head. "I am totally confused. We read Aunt Hattie's words almost every night and the dear man was mentioned several times then any mention of him just stopped, as though her mind had been blocked too. There has got to be a logical explanation for our unusual forgetfulness."

"Things that seem logical grandma, doesn't always apply to the demon world. I feel the answer to that piece of the puzzle lies somewhere in their realm. As soon as I find out the answer grandma, I will come over and we can run through all my clues and discuss our ideals like old times." Hattie chuckled. "As for letting Emily stay in my old room, you know she cannot find a single room left for miles, except room #6 in the Marshall mansion. It appears to be the only room left in town and I plan to occupy the haunted room until I find out for myself what is making all the strange noises."

"Darling, please assure Emily she is more than welcome to stay with us, for as long as she needs. It will be nice to have a young lady here with so many men running in and out." There was pure love in Nettie's voice as she added. "Tell Emily, there is only love shared here in this old farmhouse and all God's children needs a place to lay their weary head at night and have a first-class breakfast in the mornings."

"I will agree with that grandma." Hattie winked at the shy

girl who was listening in on the speaker phone.

"Hattie, about staying in that haunted room, you will be with William won't you darling? I would feel a whole lot better knowing he was there with you." Nettie was almost whispering, afraid who or what may be listening in.

"Grandma, you know how William feels about that old mansion. I haven't had time to speak to my dearest about staying yet, but whatever decision he makes will be at my best interest. I always come first where William is concerned, same as he is with me." Hattie checked her watch, knowing she had promised William to meet him at the cottage for lunch. "Grandma, you must not worry about my welfare. I am a big girl now and tangling with a ghost is a snap after facing demons. Look for Matthew and Emily. They should be getting there soon and I will pick up my little pumpkin around three."

"Alright sweet girl, but if you need me to watch Mattie while you are staying in room 6, just let me know." Nettie felt tense from all the news of ghostly sounds and the missing carriage driver. "We wouldn't want your little pumpkin to get frightened by spooky noises in the middle of night."

"Thanks for the offer grandma. I might take you up on that if William decides to stay at the mansion with me. Talk later darling." Hattie hung up, grabbed her keys, then placed Avery Torrance's letters and cards inside her large leather bag and hung it over her shoulder. Locking the small office at the far corner of Main Street, Hattie made her way quickly down the old familiar sidewalk toward the rock cottage.

CHAPTER 13

When Hattie reached the foot of the hill, she smiled at the scene before her. William Marshall was standing next to their large carriage speaking to Benson Edwards, his driver for the past fifty years. Benson had applied for the job when he was twenty-years-old and had proved to be a trusted and loyal driver, whether automobile or horse and carriage. Hattie had kept on the contended bachelor after William had departed with the Lord and it had please the owner of Marshall Mills that his faithful Hattie had been so wise to keep him as her driver.

Seeing Hattie, both gentlemen titled their hats and greeted her, both with happy smiles. William had never outgrown his old fashion manners he was accustom to from the 1800's and Hattie adored this trait about the man she loved. William Marshall was so much more charming and gallant than men were in the modern world. His old fashion ways felt right at home in the old town of Sleepy Creek, via circa 1800's. It's rough streets of brick or cobblestone where lined with 1800's buildings, each occupied by some shop or store. Several stately old homes lined Chestnut Street and the old Methodist Church, built with smooth stones and Cyprus timbers dominated the end of Grace Street and the beginning of the country road which meandered its way through beautiful woodlands and fertile fields until it came to rest at the Russel Farm. The tranquil road was perfectly named, Shady Forest.

Hattie gazed at both men, standing by the carriage, adorned with sleigh bells and chuckled softly. "William darling, you and Benson look like you just stepped out of an old Christmas card."

William laughed and patted his smiling driver on the back. "And that, my precious Hattie, was the plan. I must give all the credit to Benson for coming up with it. You know how excited the town's people are when we hold the Christmas dance at the country club and have everyone in attendance to wear 1800's clothes, thanks to your ideal before I came home to you. The one big attraction is when we drive up in the carriage. Why not use the carriage throughout the festival? Rides to and from the Marshall Mansion, to boost up all the visitors Christmas spirit and take their minds off the ghost stories."

"Darling, I think Benson has a wonderful ideal and I am sure Andrew and Shannon will appreciate such a grand addition to add to their guest's enjoyment." Hattie reached for her husband's hand and he pulled her into his arms. "I see you are all packed Benson and appear to be ready to leave for the mansion now."

"Yes ma'am. Mr. Marshall called your brother this morning and he has a room ready for me in the staff's quarters. Not to worry done, Hattie, come the night of the Christmas dance, I will be here in full 1800's attire to drive you and Mr. Marshall to the dance as always." The driver respectfully bowed and started to climb up into the driver seat when Hattie called out to him.

"Benson, if I could perhaps get you to wait around for an hour or so, until I can have lunch and a word with my husband, then maybe I will be your first guest taken up to the fine old mansion."

Respecting the ladies request, the chauffeur stepped back down, nodded politely before turning toward his employer for approval. "Sir, do you wish for me to wait on Mrs. Marshall and perhaps, you as well, sir?"

"My good man, if my wife asked for a ride, then by all means wait." William glanced down into her serious eyes. "I will hear what Hattie needs to say to me about staying at the mansion before I decide to go with her. Just go wait in your quarters and I will send Sarah out with some lunch for you." William escorted Hattie inside for some privacy. Sarah, their servant in attendance at the table, had their lunch laid out in the dining room and waited until she was dismissed, after being given orders to see to Mr. Edwards lunch. After William gave the blessing, his eyes went to his wife. "You plan to stay in room 6 darling?"

"If I am to find out what is causing the strange noises there, yes William, I see no other alternative. Darling, you know the Claxton's moved out because they were too frightened to remain at the inn. I am just grateful you found a room available in the hotel for them. Andrew paid me a visit this morning and begged me for help with this mysterious occurrence after staying in the library last night to hear for himself what others had told him." Hattie leaned forward to take his hand. "Darling, Andrew reported hearing footsteps enter the room, stop near the chair he was seated in, then continued across to the corner of the library, where Susanne's desk sat. He reported having the strange sensation he was not in the chair alone, then felt something move through him before a more-manly sound of footsteps walked in the same direction. Then there was the sound of a desk drawer opening, a soft click, like a lock being opened, then retreating footsteps."

"Then, one would assume the sounds had to be coming from some sort of ghost, haunting the old library, by Andrew's description." William felt safe at the cottage with Hattie by his side, but he did not know if he could bring himself to go back inside the mansion on the hill. "Does my smart girl have any more clues as to who it is that is haunting that old house. We both witnessed all the trapped spirits walk out behind you and leave with the Lord."

"Yes, all the ones Aunt Hattie reported as being trapped inside came out, darling. That means Pattie, Susanne, the cook, the twins, the three personal maids and Mr. Peppers, the gardener, all walked out and could never be the ghost. The butler, Mr. Rockford, alias Theodore Johnson..." Hattie made a distasteful face. "The demon, was banished from the house and he had no reason to haunt the old mansion, but that makes only eight servants when there were actually nine servants employed by you, William. So, there was one left behind, somewhere. One person everyone trapped inside the mansion had forgotten, Aunt Hattie, all the citizens of Sleepy Creek in 1814, forgot." Hattie could read confusion on her husband's handsome face. "It gets worse darling. Everyone living in Sleepy Creek today, you, my love, all my readers, and up until my new client came in, I could not remember the poor man ever existed."

"Hattie, are you saying someone was completely forgotten and left behind and now haunts the mansion?" William stood up and walked to the window, trying to sort out who the missing person was. "How can that many people just forget someone they had worked beside and saw every day? Why can't I remember a man I obviously cared for and who lived under my roof?" William turned to face his smart wife, a new revelation coming to him. "Hattie, Jesus would not have forgotten this poor lost soul. He would have called him out had he been trapped somewhere else inside the old mansion. Wouldn't He?"

"Of course, William. There is no power greater than that of our Lord." Hattie stood up and started pacing the floor. "This thought had also accrued to me, so the only explanation I can come up with is, somehow, someway, this lost spirit has the means to come and go from the mansion. On Christmas Eve in 2014, when I brought the box out, this man was nowhere around the mansion."

"Hattie dearest, you know who we forgot. Please, sweet wife, do not keep me in suspense any longer."

William was by her side in a flash, his hands firmly on her shoulders. "Tell me who has escape my memory, darling!"

"Avery Torrance! He is the poor lost soul we forgot for some unknown reason."

"Avery Torrance!" William went white and Hattie helped him in his chair. "Avery was such a good man and he worked so hard to prove himself reliable. All he ever wanted was to bring his wife Charlotte and two children to Sleepy Creek to be with him. I can still remember how happy Avery was as he helped the carpenters, in his spare time, work on the cottage I was having made for his family. It was to be finished the following spring, 1815." William rubbed his brow, wanting to unto the terrible misjustice that had befallen his carriage driver. "It is all my fault that the loving family man had to wait so long to send for them. With two failed tries at finding the right driver, I wanted to be sure I could trust and depend on Avery. After the first year I was certain he would work out, but I held back making him a permanent member of the staff until the fourth year."

"Darling, there are many things in life we would have done differently if we had the chance, but life only gives you one day at a time, and those days count off your life and go into years. There is no turning back William, we must learn to except our actions and you must never forget your actions that Christmas season was not of your own doing." Hattie had pulled her chair up next to her husband and was gently rubbing his tense shoulders. "That demon butler had you in some sort of trance and this was why he stuck by your side all those years. I believe when you heard me calling out Hattie's-Patties in the Christmas town square in 2014, your mind snapped back into reality."

"Hattie, if I had committed myself in hiring him after the first year, Avery could have been with his family the following year." William finally looked up into her eyes. "When we professed our love for one another in 2014 and I had to leave you behind, at least we got to say our farewells. That dear man not only spent four long years away from his family, but, except a few words in his last letter, Avery Torrance never got to tell his Charlotte goodbye, nor his two children. He just simply vanished."

"Yes dearest, it is sad and tragic, but if his family had been here when all of these horrible things accrued, they could have vanished too, and with no one alive to report them missing, that family would have been simply forgotten." Hattie walked over to get the carriage driver's last letter to his wife and held it up.

"As for Avery's last letter to Charlotte, there are a little more than a few words in here."

"That is Susanne's stationary. I recognized it immediately." Then, it dawned on him why the driver hadn't used his stationary as was his custom. William dropped his head, feeling remorseful. "Avery had always come to me for writing paper because I had happily offered to supply all he needed to keep in touch with his wife. On the last occasion when he asked for a few sheets, I jumped him, asking him if I didn't pay him enough money to buy his own stationary. I…I just had so much weighing on my mind! I felt myself going crazy! Hattie, I knew Avery Torrance would never live to see his family again. I assume he would be trapped inside the mansion like everyone else. I had given him the rest of the evening off, so he would have gone inside, for dinner, to read in the library, play checkers with his friend, Lucas Peppers, maybe retire to his room early only to get shut inside forever! So, when he asked for the paper, I lost it! My immediate response was to tell Avery to saddle one of my horses and go back to Charlotte and his children, but I quickly withdrew those thoughts when I spotted the demon watching me. I had to just walk away, making my life even more miserable."

"Sweetheart, I don't want this case to upset you by bringing back all these unwanted memories." Hattie put her arms around him for comfort. "But if I am every going to solve this mystery and find out the truth about Avery Torrance so his spirit can be set free to go to heaven and finally reunite with Charlotte and his children, then I must ask you some important questions that only you are capable of answering."

"My darling Hattie, I know the smart detective that lives inside that fabulous body of yours will not rest until you solve this mystery. To be honest, precious, I too wish to find Avery Torrance's body and find out just what happened to him on December 24,1814."

Hattie smiled and gave her husband a loving kiss which lasted a little longer when William pulled her over into his arms. "I shall miss those romantic kisses while I am away searching for ghost." She laughed when he tickled her waist."

"I never said I would not go, now, did I, Mrs. Marshall?" he nuzzled her neck.

"No, you did not William. But I know you pretty well and I'm not sure you are ready to go back inside that mansion at night, but I do need you to come by in the morning to go over the original layout of the home's interior." Hattie stood up and felt William's hand give her rear a light spank. She giggled and started pacing.

"Avery did get his letter off to Charlotte and it was several pages long. He never got to tell her goodbye in person, but the disturbed man same as told his wife goodbye, sensing his life was about to be cut short." Hattie's attention fell on the husband. "William, Susanne's desk always set in the far corner of the library, so that answers why the footsteps walked over in that direction. Do you remember which chair Avery always sat in while he read?"

"He liked the big armchair that sat next to the library door." William recalled passing the library while going through the central hallway to the dining room and seeing his chauffeur lost in a good book."

"That makes sense, since he could hear the conversation between you and Rockford very clearly in the hallway." Hattie noticed her husband's hand tremble so she walked over and sat down in his lap. The trembling vanished as he wrapped his arms around her waist, thankful for her compassion for him. "Yes darling, that was when Mr. Torrance grew suspicious of something unusual happening, as did your daughter Pattie."

"Pattie? Pattie had suspicions about me?" A tear ran down William's cheek as he searched his mind for any clue of her mistrust in the man she had always looked up to and loved. "I cannot recall any difference in my daughter's affection for me."

"Pattie loved you darling and no matter what happened to her, she never stopped missing or loving her daddy." Hattie gave his wet cheek a kiss, then let her mind wonder. "After the ghost reached the desk, Andrew heard a drawer open then a click. I recall Susanne's desk had three drawers on either side and one large drawer in the middle. Can you remember where her secret door was on the desk?"

"Hattie, how on earth did you uncover that hidden clue?" William looked at her remarkable deduction. "Susanne insisted on a large desk and it must contain some sort of hidden compartment. All the other desk we looked at had one secret drawer. The desk we decided to buy had two hidden drawers and one well-hidden mini closet, with an invisible door, secured by a built-in lock, camouflaged among the intriguing pattern." He thought about the small size of the hidden compartments and shook his head.

"Hattie, Susanne could not have kept her boxes of stationary in either of the secret compartments, so, she must have given Avery something else. Something she prized and was very special to her."

"That's right darling. Your wife gave Avery one of her keepsake Christmas cards to give Charlotte. The perfect card he had been searching for, but he never had the chance to mail it. So, wherever Avery Torrance ended up, the missing Christmas card will be found."

William arose slowly and walked to the window to stare out at the big carriage and a set of new white horses. Since the terrible night in 1814, William Marshall had bought several replacement carriage horses, always white. He had lost count of the number of fine horses that grew to old to pull the heavy carriages. William had never asked his evil butler what he had done with the previous horses, but he felt certain the evil man did not have mercy on them and put them out to pasture.

Staring out at the scene he remembered the last time he had spent with Mr. Torrance. "It was my fault the Christmas card was never mailed. I needed Avery's help one more time and his friend Lucas Peppers told me where I could find him. In the stables, preparing to take his friend's horse to town in time to get the card off before the mail clerk closed for the holidays." William took a deep breath, finding it hard to breathe. Hattie walked over and wrapped her arms around his trembling shoulders. "I needed Avery to hook up the big carriage for me. I needed it for all my things I had to get out of the house before..., I asked him to take it to the side door. I did not want Susanne or Pattie to see me carry out all those suitcases and hide them, for...my get away." This time the tears flowed down his cheeks as he spoke. "I was helpless when it came to hooking up the big carriage and Avery was the best carriage driver I had ever had and I knew he would choose helping me over his own personal problems. Hattie, I was like a mad man. I did not know why I could not stop myself, even though inside I wanted to make it all go away, but it was too late. The demons were in charge of my body and they made me kill my family and everyone living inside my home!" he broke down in his wife's arms.

"William, I feel this is going to be too hard for you darling, so I will understand if you had rather not come to the mansion at all." She caressed his head gently. "Before the mansion became a bed and breakfast, I went to the mansion with daddy and grandpa, so if I walk around inside the mansion things may come back to me along with my recurring dream when I was ten."

"My girl's been having nightmares about that mansion?" William regained control and pulled Hattie into his arms. "Sweetheart, I will not let you down, nor will I let Avery Torrance down again. I promise to be there in the morning to help you with the layout and whatever you need. I would even bring myself to spending tonight with you if I hadn't told Mr. Jackson, the Mill manager I would meet with him later tonight after the mill closes. If my clever sleuth hasn't solved the mystery by tomorrow night, I will be bringing my pajamas over and join you in room 6, one of my servant's old rooms."

"Good deduction William. I must be rubbing off on you." Hattie laughed, glad to know she would be seeing her true love in the morning and perhaps the following night. "The male ghost we might encounter will be Avery Torrance and room 6 was his room over 200 years ago. As for the lady's footsteps, that is a puzzle, because we both saw Susanne leave with Jesus, so she cannot be a ghost. I guess I might find the answer this evening, then again at midnight, when the clock in the central hallway strikes twelve." She reached up and kissed her husband "I must pack and call grandma about keeping Mattie for us like she offered. Then I'm off in my carriage, to make a grand entrance to the mansion on the hill."

CHAPTER 14

As the carriage winded its way up the long driveway to the Marshall mansion, Benson Edwards could not contain his statement any longer. "Hattie, please except my apology for going over your head and asking for Mr. Marshall's approval when you ask me to wait for you."

"Benson, there is nothing to apologize for. I realized you worked for William long before I inherited all his personal belongings." Hattie reached over and patted the driver's back. "Now that William is back, he is in his rightful place as owner and husband. I appreciate his old fashion beliefs that the husband makes the final decisions for his family. William is a good judge of what is right for the two of us and little Mattie."

"I still feel grateful for everything you did for me when you suddenly inherited Mr. Marshall's great fortune, including his staff of workers." Mr. Edwards looked over with admiration. "Even at ten-years-old, your kind heart kept on every staff member William had working for him. I shall never forget your generosity in our pay, weather you needed us or not. Believe me Hattie, everyone in staff think the world of you and that is why I felt like some sort of traitor for going over your head to ask your husband."

"It was the right thing to do Benson. As for keeping the staff, I knew I would be moving in the cottage soon and I wanted things to remain just as it had been with William." Hattie saw the big mansion looming on the hill. "You were with William for several years before I came to know him."

"Yes ma'am, this month I turned seventy-years-old, making it fifty years driving for Mr. Marshall." The driver slowed the team of horses down as they drew closer and saw guest sitting in the big porch watching the big carriage and four white horses with excitement. "Begging your pardon, ma'am, but before you came into Mr. Marshall's life, he wasn't the easiest person to work for. He was demanding, arrogant, and there were times when he threatened to fire me if his commands where not met. I can see a big change in my employer since he met you." Benson glanced over, still looking apologetic. "I guess when you ask me to wait on you, I feared the old Mr. Marshall would come out, after telling me before you stepped up, to take my leave with the carriage. So, I must sincerely apologize."

"Then if it means that much to you Benson, your apology, although it's not necessary, is excepted. You are forgiven." Hattie gave him her reassuring smile when he helped her down, then retrieved her piece of luggage. "Have fun impressing the guest, Benson." She waved at her brother when he stepped out to see why all the guest were so excited. "Alright Andrew, I am ready to tour the house.

Hattie made her way up the back staircase, cut off to paying guest due to the steep risers. This part of the mansion seemed to be untouched by the renovation and old cobwebs made it clear the cleaning crew never ventured down these corridors. The dim lamps on the wall had never been upgraded to modern lighting and their flickering gave off an eerier glow. As she made her way slowly up, she mumbled to herself.

"If these steps are not used anymore, then where do they come out. Being the old servant's steps, one must assume the steps rose to the third floor. Perhaps a common hallway, which is now the hallway to the guest on the west side." Hattie stopped when she reached the end of the stairs and a closed door. "This old door has either been sealed off from the third-floor hallway or locked from the inside." Her fingers gripped the old doorknob and found it would not budge. "So, it is locked from inside and the key is missing. I will check the upper hallway and see if this door is still there or if the carpenters sealed it off with a wall." As her hand ran along the smooth wood on the old door she thought. "I wonder...when the clock strikes midnight, will this old staircase become as it was four hundred years ago and if so, will this door open and what will I find on the other side?"

Hattie made sure she would be alone in the library to hear for herself the same sounds Andrew had reported hearing the night before. Sitting in the soft armchair where Andrew confirmed he had used the previous night, proving what William had told her during their lunch, the bright detective could hear conversations made by the inn's guest on their way to the dining room. So, Avery Torrance could have easily made out the conversation between her husband and the satanic butler. As the diners left for the night's activities in town square, Hattie could sense the stillness closing in on her, making her a little apprehensive of what lied ahead.

A sudden crick on the wooden floor brought her to full attention, then the definite sound of footsteps, those of a woman wearing heels. The unmistakable sensation of movement beneath her before the being stood up, passing right through her body. Hattie shook off the unnatural feeling and stood up slowly, following the other footsteps, those of a tall man. She perked up her ears for any words passed between the beings but could hear nothing but one of the desk drawers opening. With her keen senses, the smart detective concluded it was the middle drawer closes to her, although it remained closed, unlike her dream. She stepped closer to hear the click and to Hattie's surprise, she saw a small key float up and placed itself into one of the pattern squares, then it made a clicking noise and vanished. The footsteps retreated then silence.

Hattie walked around the big desk and took a seat before pulling out the middle drawer. It held several boxes of unused stationary with matching envelopes. She lifted out one box to examine closely and discovered it was the exact paper Avery Torrance had used to write his last letter to his wife Charlotte. Hattie had noticed it was the only blue stationary in the big tied-up bundle Emily Torrance had handed her.

"The missing Christmas card had to come from the secret mini closet, but where could the key be?" Hattie felt around the square patterns for a metal keyhole in the area where she had watched in wonder the floating key. "Susanne most likely kept the key on her person at all times, so after they were locked inside, would she have held the possessions inside that secret compartment as special as she once did, or would she have taken the key out of her pocket and tossed it aside somewhere. "Hattie searched the desktop thoroughly, then all six drawers and found no sign of a tiny key. "Just suppose Susanne had kept the key on her person and it was with her the day she died. There was nothing left but the skeleton remains of those that died over two hundred years ago, huddled together. The key is metal, so it would not deteriorate like cloth or flesh, so it had to be someplace where the bodies had been found. She knew she must wait until the following morning before she could search the area, so for now Hattie would wait until the clock struck twelve and see if the ghost of Avery Torrance would appear in room number six.

CHAPTER 15

Offering to place a rollaway bed in her room where he could join her, Andrew was graciously turned down by his strong will sister. "Andrew, you are very sweet to think about my welfare, but I can assure you I am perfectly capable of handling a ghost." Hattie reached up on her tip toes to kiss her older brother. "You were always my protecting brother, always looking out for your baby sister, but I feel your wife Shannon needs your presence at bedtime far more than I do."

"Shannon has been jumpy lately. Any little sound brings her into my arms." Andrew smiled. "But if you should need me during the night Hattie, please come wake me up. I would feel a whole lot better if William were with you."

William has promised to come tomorrow morning to help me with the old floor plans and then stay with me tomorrow night." Hattie raised her shoulders in doubt. "I'm not sure William is ready to spend the night in his old home. Too many bad memories, not to mention his feeling guilty over Avery Torrance's disappearance and the cold fact that nobody remembered he every excised, including him."

"I have faith in you sis, so whatever you think best, I will stand by your decision."

Room 6 lay on the far in of the third-floor hallway, separated some distance from the other eight servant rooms, now opened up for more spacious bedrooms with a connecting bathroom. Where there had been four doors across from the other four doors back the old 1804 layout, with the ninth servant's room door, belonging Mr. Torrance, at the end, the new B&B consisted of two doors facing the other two doors with the larger suite, room 6, more private at the end of the wide hallway. A total of five guest suites. Three on the west side and two on the north side, with matching suites on the second floor. The new set of stairs continued from the second floor as it swept up with more elegance to the third floor and rest directly in the middle of the wide hallway, dividing the west side and the north side. The second and third floors had a total of ten guest suites between them and all where full except for room 6.

It had grown late after talking to her brother, calling Nettie to check on Mattie, then the lengthy conversation with William. The lights along the hallway on the third floor had already gone dim, with the automatic timing system, so it gave off an eyrie glow, as objects in the hallway, like potted ferns or wall table lamps cast shadows of odd shapes. Hattie thought "Most people would be frightened walking down this corridor this time of night. Everyone is preparing for bed or already asleep after a busy day with the festival." Hattie stopped, contemplating her last word, festival. This was the first year in her life she had not participated at a single event. Her mind had been so wrapped up with completing her last case so she would be free to enjoy the entire Christmas season, but knowing Avery Torrance was still missing, Hattie felt somehow responsible. She had assumed the Mystery of the Marshall Mansion had been resolved, but until she found out what happen to that sweet man that never got to spend another Christmas with his wife and children, she would have to leave the festival fun to everyone else. She would attend the games to root for her brothers and the Brower's against those Caswell cheaters. Hattie smiled, thinking about dancing in her husband's arms. "And nothing will keep me from going to the dance with William." She said softly.as she came close to the last room, freezing in her tracks when she heard the sound of a soft drawn-out whisper. "William."

It was distinctly a male, but who? What? She thought as the clock struck twelve and she noticed at the end of the hall, shadowed in darkness, the solid wall began wavering until an old oak door appeared. Blinking twice, thinking her fatigue was causing her to hallucinate, she walked over and tried the knob. It opened to the dreary old servant's steps she had discovered earlier that day. Feeling a draft of wind blow up a musty smell from the shut-off halls below, she quickly closed the door and turn to go inside her guest room. There was something different about the door when she had brought her bag up after arriving. After studying the obvious difference, she knew this door belonged to the 1800's. Too unnerved to check out the rest of the hallway for eight doors instead of four, she put her key back in the bag, knowing it wouldn't fit, and tried the doorknob. With deliberate slow movements, she opened the door and tried to focus in the dark room that smelled like a man's pipe. Hattie noticed a dim light at the window, the moon shining through a small opening in what looked like shutters.

"The noise always started when the clock struck midnight." Hattie thought to herself as she listened for any sounds over by the window, where the ghost by now was peering out at the garden below. Trying to decide which side of the window Avery stood at, she could slip over and peek out from the opposite side. She thought as she walked over, trying not to make a sound. "Those demons looked straight up at Mr. Torrance in December 22, 1814. I wonder, if I look out and see them, will they see me watching as well?" Hattie shook the bad thought off and peeped down, gasping when she saw William talking to the invisible thing and Mr. Rockford.

Hattie held her breath, unsure if the spirit by the window had heard her gasp after seeing her husband back in 1814. She soon found out when she felt a warm hand push her away from the window before the demons looked up. Avery Torrance had just saved her from being seen by the demons.

Hattie closed her eyes as she took a deep breath, and when she opened them she was back in the present time's bedroom suite.

CHAPTER 16

William had arrived early the next morning, just as he had promised. He had spent his first night without his true love lying beside him and he had missed her terribly. If she had not found all she had come after, then somehow, he would bring himself to stay with her in room 6, his servant's old quarters. Over coffee they discussed their night apart.

"Both the library and room 6 proved active last night. I witnessed everything Andrew described in the library but my experience on the third floor was something completely different than the Claxton's described." Hattie looked down at her cup, unsure how William would take what she was about to say. "After speaking to Andrew, grandma, then you, my darling, it was late when I went up to the third floor. Things took on a different atmosphere at quarter till twelve. The dim hallway cast ghostly shadows along the corridor and I was thinking how others might grow tense by such a passage. Then my thoughts went to the festival and my lack of participation, and my determination to go to the winter games. Then I declared softly to myself, "And nothing will keep me from going to the dance with William." Hattie felt his arm circle her waist, before he whispered.

"Our private table my darling and all the dances you desire."

Hattie smiled up, before continuing. "When I said your name darling, I distinctly heard a male voice repeat your name very softly." William pulled away and looked into her eyes, almost fearing what she might say next. "William, I noticed the wall at end of the hallway give way to a very old door. I opened it and saw the servant's steps I had walked up earlier that day. I quickly closed it and started to go inside my room. Darling, somehow, I found myself back in 1814 and room 6 had turned back into Avery Torrance bedroom. I smelled his pipe, and from the partly open shutters, knew our ghost was standing by the window." Hattie noticed William's hands trembling as she took them. "Darling, if you rather not hear the rest, I will understand."

"It won't change the fact that you saw the garden below Hattie. Besides me standing there making that foolish deal with the devil, did you get caught watching by those demons, like poor Avery did?" William remembered the horrible details of his carriage driver's last letter.

"No, they never saw me, thanks to Avery Torrance, who had heard me gasp when I saw you below and he pushed me out of the way before they could look up." Hattie could tell William was getting upset so she knew she must somehow talk him into staying at the cottage yet another night without her. "Darling, I am not upset by what I saw below in the garden. It was just seeing the man I love so upset and tortured from the 1800's that startled me for a moment. "I understand why you should not stay in this house at night, my dearest William. I appreciate the deep memories that have lived with you for so many years before the Lord forgave you and gave us another chance to be together."

"I do not wish to be without you by my side again, my Hattie. The cottage is a lonely place without you and I have nightmares of Theodore Johnson returning to take up where he left off." William held her tightly in his arms. "Please, let me stay with you darling. Even with all the bad memories that live within these walls, just being near you will ease the stress from our being apart."

"William, you know I will honor whatever choice you make, darling, and should we go to bed early, make passionate love so you can fall into a restful sleep, then at the strike of twelve, God willing, I will be the only one to wake and hear the ghost." Hattie's smile matched his. "And there's no need to worry, should I find myself back in 1814. I will not give those demons a chance to see me."

"Hattie, if room 6 becomes Avery's room, where will I be sleeping?" William felt strange over the apparition his wife had witness and he wondered if the room could be both places at the same time."

"I feel we will be in the same room, but for a short time I will be in the 1814 bedroom while you are sleeping in the 2025 bedroom." Hattie realized how strange her statement sounded but she didn't have any other explanation.

"Hattie darling, promise me, you will not get stuck in the 1814 bedroom!" William asked her seriously'

"I recall hearing an apparition only last a few minutes before you return to the present." Hattie needed for her husband not to worry about her and lose sleep, only to find himself back in his 1814 nightmare. "Now, the reason I've ask you to help me this morning before you leave for work." The sooner she got his mind off the ghostly past, the better, Hattie thought. "I need for you to show me where the music room was, to see if the library is as it was in 1814, and the west side of the third floor, partially the lay-out of the servant's quarters."

William clutched Hattie's hand tightly as he led her down the central hall to a closed door on the first floor. He stared for a moment at the new wall, then looked across at the familiar drawing room he had sat in many times before his fatal mistake in 1814. "I recall the music room was straight across the hallway from the formal drawing room, still in the exact spot. I assume the Mr. Claxton that transformed my mansion into the B&B, is the same Claxton that stayed in room 6 before the ghost ran him and his wife out."

"Yes darling, Mr. Claxton was my architect." Hattie looked at the single door flanked by walls, covered in delicate flowered wallpaper. "So, the music room would have been just inside this door."

"Only there wasn't a door at the time, just a big arch like the drawing room has." William opened the door and found a big deep closet, filled with extra chairs near the entrance. "I assume the plan called for the adjacent room to be bigger so they took part of the music room and had the remainder left a catch all closet."

"I wonder if the piano is still somewhere inside the closet. Perhaps, along the back wall." Hattie knew she must search the closet as well as the adjacent room's far right side for any sign of the key. "I'll return later and search for Susanne's tiny secret closet key. I am sure if the clean-up crew didn't sweep it up with the sawdust it will be found in the music room area." She led her husband down the hallway passed the grandfather clock to the library.

After looking around the big room, William walked over to his first wife's desk, still sitting at the same spot he last saw his wife at. Tears filled his eyes as he recalled their last words before he left the house and his loving family for the last time.

"William, please promise me that you will be back in time for church services tonight. Your daughter has been anxious by your recent behavior and you must, at least for Pattie's sake, come back and take us as a family. The family she remembers." Susanne had been writing last minute invitations to their annual New Year's party when her husband came in the library to say he was leaving for the office. "William, I'm not sure what has happened to us, but I would like nothing more than to make our marriage work. Please darling, can we try. I still love you dearly."

"Susanne, I never stopped loving you. I've just been going through some rough times. Your asking for a divorce hasn't help any." William remembered how he wanted to grab her hand and get Pattie. Then escape with them both, but his intentions were stopped when the butler stepped inside and ushered him away, without even a farewell to the family he loved. "Writing useless New Year invitations." he mumbled aloud, and Hattie stepped up beside him.

"William, I cannot help but feel you are remembering your first wife at this moment, not that I blame you darling. I know you loved Susanne and perhaps you are recalling your last moments together before you left for good." Hattie could feel

Joan Byrd

her heart ache for her husband. "I should never have asked you to come back inside your old mansion. It has brought back memories you had tucked away inside your head. Darling, if it's too painful to continue, I will understand. Just walking around, I can recall how things looked when daddy and grandpa came with me after you were gone."

"My most-dearest Hattie, you always were of a pure heart. Never did you get jealous over my love for Susanne and Pattie." William pulled his wife into a warm embrace and kissed her with passion. "I learned a lot about love from a ten-year-old girl who stole my heart and changed me for the better. My little angel that saved my soul and snatched me out of the devil's claws. The child of God that helped me set my family and dear servants free after two-hundred-years. No one could ever replace you in my heart Hattie Russel Marshall. The only one I love more is our Lord, Father, Son, and Holy Spirit." William gave her another kiss. "I was recalling my last moments with Susanne and was ready to take her and Pattie with me and run, but that demon Rockford stopped me."

"Those demons have a lot of power once they get their victim under their control and for some familiar feeling, I cannot help but believe they still have their power over Avery Torrance." Hattie had the nagging sensation that because she remembered Avery and was searching for answers, the demons had returned to Sleepy Creek. "William, we must be vigilant at all times and beware of any strangers in our mist."

"Hattie, you believe the demons have returned, don't you? Be honest with me." William had turned her around to face him, the need to know what she was thinking.

"Darling, there's no other way for Avery Torrance to have been erased from everyone's memories other than a powerful angel's gift." Hattie took his hands in hers. "William, I haven't had the opportunity to speak to Reverend Westly yet, but he is well versed in the origins of God's angels and he might agree with my assumption that angels have the power to block a human's mind, the gift meant for good intentions when the

84

Creator handed them this power. The fallen angels have found the means to turn the beautiful gift into another way to control God's children, such as Theodore Johnson did you when he took on the role as Clarence Rockford."

"So, this same demon, could be posing as someone else?"

"Even animals if it suits their cause." Hattie led her husband to the unused back hallway to show him the old servant's steps. "Sleepy Creek is bursting with festival visitors, and many are new to our town so the demons could be posing as anyone, even children." She stopped at the musty old steep flight of stairs and William instantly recalled standing at the bottom waiting for his carriage driver to come down.

"I stood in this very spot waiting for Avery Torrance to descend down the stairs so I could ask him to hook up the small carriage for me. I could handle one horse with no trouble and navigating around the crowd wasn't as dangerous." William thought back to the time and remembered the reason very clearly after 211years. "I wanted Pattie to come down to the office so I could spend some precious time with her. I tried to act cheerful and normal, but I knew soon I would never see my beautiful little girl ever again. My heart was breaking! I wanted to hide her away so Rockford couldn't find her, then somehow get Susanne and my loyal workers out of the house. That demon butler was always one step ahead of me and they had sworn if I try anything to break the bargain I would die instantly and be taken to everlasting punishment." William felt Hattie's embrace and he held her tightly. "They had me trapped darling. I was scared of dying until I met you and found the greatest love a man could find. I wasn't afraid to die anymore. I was sad about leaving you after I had found you, only at the time, it was too late for us." William caressed her face. "To have received the gift of a second chance with you from our loving Lord was a Christmas miracle and I can promise you, my dearest love, I will never let you down, demons or no demons! I saw what faith can do from that small ten-year-old girl I fell in love with, and the power of the Almighty God will be our sword and shield against anything Lucifer throws at us!"

Hattie saw a stronger William Marshall standing smiling down at her, suddenly unafraid to help her fight for what was right and to find and save Avery Torrance and finally set him free. He had faced his past memories head on and William had found strength in the Lord Jesus, whom he had seen and walked with in heaven.

"William, welcome aboard the missing piece team! Now, to the servant's quarters!" Knowing the old servant's stairs were cut off, the couple walked up the center staircase to the third floor and William looked up and down the hallway, trying to recall the 1804 floor plan. "Darling, I remember eight rooms, four on either side of the hall, across from each other with Avery Torrance's at the far end alone."

"You are right Hattie. Lucas Peppers and Clarence Rockford had the far end rooms facing each other. Mable Folly, the cook, had the room next to Rockford, and across from her was Rose Redding, Susanne's personal maid. The twins, Milly and Tilly Shields had adjoining rooms side by side and the rooms across from them were, Pattie's personal maid, Joyce Ann Goodyear and my personal maid, Velda Turner." William had remembered taking the staff up when they arrived to show them where they would stay. He recalled how excited they were to have such elaborate rooms. "The staff were very pleased with their living arrangements and the women felt safe having the men at both ends of the hallway."

"I'm just glad to know which room belonged to Rockford, in case I travel back to 1814." Hattie led the way to the other end. "I will avoid that end of the hall and concentrate on Avery's room."

"Make that we, darling. You do not have to go through this alone from now on." William draped his arm around her protectively as they walked inside their room. "This is more elegant than Avery's room was. There was one single bed in the far corner, a small vanity with a mirror, a single chair, washstand containing a wash basin and pitcher. I recall Avery enjoyed a pipe and kept it on the vanity with his pouch of pipe tobacco." He walked around trying to remember anything else that was different. "Oh yes, he asked for a small writing desk that sat near the window and…" William walked over and looked down into the garden adorned with Christmas decorations "there was a small candle stand on the desk and shutters on the window."

"That's some kind of memory Mr. Marshall." Hattie reached up and gave him a kiss. "It was dark when I came inside the 1804 room last night so I was too late to hear the spirit slip from bed, which would have been the squeaking sound the Claxton's heard before the footsteps moving toward the window. Like I said, I smelled a pipe, so it had to be Avery in the room with me."

"And that is another reason I should be with you darling, in case the lonely ghost mistakes you for his wife, Charlotte." William gave her a playful wink. "But seriously, should this room return to the 1814's, I would feel better if I were with you to save you this time from looking down in that spooky garden."

"Last night could have just been a freaky occurrence and might not return for us to witness." Hattie walked over and gazed down at the tranquil scene below, much different than the previous night. "I will pay grandma a visit to check on Mattie, then go see Reverend Westly at one. I called him right before you got here and made the appointment."

"I could work from the cottage if you want to bring Mattie over for an early lunch, around eleven." William wrapped his arms around Hattie, then gave her a kiss. "I'll have the cook prepare our lunch and afterwards, Mattie can stay with me until its time to come back here for the night. I will run her by the farm on my way."

"That, my darling William, sounds like a splendid ideal." They walked hand in hand down to the front door and kissed one more time before William walked out to his car, waved and drove away. Checking her watch, Hattie knew the music room would have to wait until she returned to search for the tiny key, if it should still be there. She made herself a mental note to search the desk for the New Years invitations Susanne had been writing when William last saw her. But the main thing Hattie wanted to find was the box of Christmas cards hidden inside the locked mini closet to see if they were numbered. If so, Avery Torrance had one of the cards. Was the missing Christmas card number 1 in Susanne's private collection? Hattie knew if she found the missing card, she would find the missing man.

CHAPTER 17

"How was your night in the Russel farmhouse Emily?" Hattie had arrived as the Russel's houseguest was finishing her big breakfast."

"Your family is divine, Hattie. The men folk are charming and your mother Carolyn and Grandma Nettie, are super women. Hard working too, the entire family." Emily Torrance sipped on her second cup of coffee and chuckled to herself. "If I stay here much longer, I will be as big as Nettie's stove. She wasn't fibbing when she said the best breakfast around. Her lunch and supper are wonderful too."

"I could not agree more. My grandma makes the best everything, including conversations." Hattie glanced up the stairs. "The dear woman insisted I stay and chat with you while she gets my little pumpkin ready to go visit her papa." Hattie got up to pour herself a cup of the good smelling coffee, then grabbed a cookie out of the Nettie's cookie factory jar. "Have you had the chance to try one of my Hattie's-Patties?"

"I must admit I have sampled every cookie Nettie's cookie factory has to offer." Emily lifted up a hidden cookie from beside her plate. "I think I'll join you." She crunched down before asking "Have you found out anything yet about Grandfather Torrance?"

"Actually, your grandfather saved me last night." Hattie smiled when Emily almost got strangled.

"Grandpa...saved you? But...how?"

"I guess because I went up to my room right before midnight, I was swept back to 1814 and when I realized Mr. Torrance was standing at the window looking down in the garden, I slipped over to have a peek. I foolishly let out a gasp when I saw my husband standing below speaking to both demons and knowing it was William in 1814, not my present

William. I held my breath, hoping the ghost hadn't heard me when suddenly I felt his hand push me away from the window before the demons looked up."

"Hattie Russel! What, in the name of God, where you doing in that spooky room?" Nettie walked up in time to hear Hattie relive her midnight adventure. "If you were transferred back to 1814, what makes you think Mr. Torrance was a ghost? He was very much alive in 1814 and I think that is why the dear man could push you out of the way."

"Come to think of it grandma, the hand that pushed me to safety was warm." Hattie stood up and joined Nettie, holding Mattie, watching her mama with big brown eyes. "If Avery was alive last night, I could have spoken to him and he could have helped me with some questions I have."

"I am certain he could not have helped you know where he was missing, if he were reliving December 22." Emily joined in the conversation, recalling his statements in the letter. "Grandfather could have told you about William's unusual behavior, not wanting to give him stationary to write Grandma Charlotte, borrowing stationary from Susanne and her giving him the Christmas card."

"Yes, he could have told me all about the Christmas card and where Susanne had her key to the hidden door in the desk." Hattie paced the kitchen floor. "I would have asked about the conversation between William and the butler outside the library door, but I am certain my time would have been limited. After he pushed me out of the way, I was back in the presence."

"What did you do to go back in time, Hattie darling? Did you, touch anything that could have triggered time to change?" Nettie put Mattie in her highchair and handed her a cookie. "You must have done something to cause time to reverse."

"I was walking down the dim hallway toward my room, number 6, thinking about the festival and going to the dance with William…" Hattie felt the lightbulb go off inside her head. "William! I said his name softly and that's when I heard a male voice repeat his name in a whisper. The solid wall in front of me began to waver, then an old door appeared at the end of the hallway. I opened it and saw the old servant's staircase I had discovered earlier, but then the door would not budge. The musty odor caused me to shut it and when I started to open my room door, I noticed the entrance door wasn't the one I had seen that afternoon." Hattie stopped pacing and glanced at her grandma. "I think the secret to the past was when I said William as the clock below struck midnight."

Hattie had enjoyed her time with William and Mattie, and at one p.m. she waited in Reverend Westly's office. She glanced around at the paintings on the church study walls, mostly those of angels. She walked over to a row of high-ranking angels and recognized Michael defeating Lucifer during the battle for heaven. "What we need to defeat you again Lucifer, is the strength of Michael!" Hattie hadn't noticed the pastor walk in and listen to her statement.

"Hattie, is your instincts pointing toward the old dragon's return to Sleepy Creek?" Seeing the seriousness on her pretty face, he joined her at the wall. "In times of human need, sometimes God will send his angels to protect us from his old foe. If the enemy is strong enough to do damage to one belonging to the Lord, the Creator will send the powerful warrior angels to do the fighting for you. There is no demon brave enough to take on the powerful warriors." Reverend Westly gathered Hattie's hand in his. "I recall the last battle you waged with one of Lucifer's demons, the Lord Jesus Himself came to your defense."

"The Lord had lost sheep to take home to heaven then, Reverend Westly. It appears there was one lost sheep left behind and it is this man I seek to find for Jesus." Hattie noticed the puzzled look on her minister's face. "You cannot recall the one left behind because, like me and everyone else, your mind was blocked by some powerful force."

"And you believe it had something to do with those demons, the fallen angels that went with Lucifer." The pastor motioned toward the chair in front of his desk as he took down a big book, titled: The Powers of God's Angels, and sat it on his desk before sitting down. "Angels are gifted in many things that are meant to help serve the Creator Himself or in many cases, human beings. The gift you refer to belongs to the guardian angels. Those men angels that watch over every child born to God's family. It is thought each person's guardian can be seen while they are very young and as the child grows, the loving angel blocks their memory of him so he or she can grow up and live their lives. There have been cases when the angel once again reveals himself to his adult ward, such as a writer whose words come from their devoted guardian."

"So, these demons that blocked everyone's memory about Avery Torrance, the carriage driver..." Hattie smiled when Mr. Westly sat up in shock, recalling the chauffeur. "Had to be future guardian angels before they were thrown out of heaven. A gift meant for good reversed for evil."

"Very good deduction, Hattie." Reverend Westly closed the thick book. "It would appear that is exactly what happened. Do you have any clues as to where Mr. Torrance's body can be hidden?"

"Not so far Jim, but clues are piling up." Hattie stood up and put on her wool coat. "I feel the demons are back in Sleepy Creek and they could be impersonating as anyone new to town. We must all be on alert for any unusual happenings during the festival. I must admit, this case has kept me tied up and the festival has taken second place. I feel its time for me to start mingling with the crowd and see what I can pick up."

"Just be careful out there Hattie. Demons can prove very dangerous when they feel caught in their act, and knowing your talent for solving a mystery, they are surely watching your moves." The minister walked his young friend to the door. "Call me if you need me and if I should sense their presence, I will get in touch."

"Thanks Jim. Just promise me you will be careful as well." Hattie hugged her old friend. "If demons are as smart as you say, they probably know your knowledge of their powers."

Hattie had informed William about her visit with the minister and said she would wait on him at the B&B for dinner. In the meantime, she had a key to find. After pulling the stacked chairs out in the hallway, Hattie walked back to what was the remainder of the music room. Other than the chairs near the door, Hattie thought most of the music room still remained intact, as much as she recalled when Andrew had brought her back to the mansion to find the remains of the nine victims trapped inside for 200 years.

January 10, 2015 "Pattie said we would find their remains all huddled together in the music room." Ten-year-old Hattie Russel had told her brother as they walked inside the dim entrance hall.

"Do you know where the music room is Hattie? This is a big house and it still feels a little spooky after all that happened here." Andrew held his sister's hand and marveled at how steady it felt.

"There's really nothing here to be afraid of any longer Andrew." Hattie smiled up, remembering how Mr. Johnson, the demon butler just vanished from the steps when she had felt Jesus banish him away. "On Christmas Eve, I stepped inside a very dark house, barely lit by the full moon overhead outside. I heard music coming from someplace on the north side of the house and it suddenly stopped when Bart Bower walked up and startled me when he touched my shoulder. I let out a soft scream, then the music stopped. With eyes wide in fear, Bart asked if I had just been playing music." Hattie rolled up her eyes in discuss. "Bart started talking brave until Pattie's ghost appeared on the steps and said Hattie, thinking I was Aunt Hattie."

"Aunt Hattie did mention hearing music coming from the music room." Andrew had read the old diary for himself after getting intrigued over the mystery. "I recall she heard her friend Pattie singing a Christmas carol in there as well."

"O Holy Night, the same song her mother was playing when Aunt Hattie just heard music as well as me and Bart."

Joan Byrd

Hattie started leading Andrew down the central hallway passed the silent grandfather clock, that had not been wound in many years. They found the music room directly across from the formal drawing room, later called the formal living room "There's the grand-piano." Ten-year-old Hattie walked over and ran her fingers down the keys, causing years of dust to float up in their face. "Sorry Andrew, I forgot about the built-up dust." They laughed after they both stopped sneezing.

Andrew pulled Hattie back when he noticed a pile of bones behind the piano. "Don't look sis, I have found the remains and I think it's best if you remember those lovely people the last time you saw them, going home with Jesus."

"I guess there's nothing left but bones after 200 years. Maybe scraps of cloth among the huddled-up bones." Hattie could not control her jitters thinking about the sad scene behind the piano."

Present time: "Behind the piano! Susanne's body would have been somewhere behind her piano and if she had the key on her, say, in a pocket, it could still be someplace back there since most of the room still looks like it did when Andrew and I was here." Hattie stepped to the back, glad to find all the remains had been recovered. She got down on her knees and felt around under the piano's claw feet. Hattie was disappointed to find only dust. After a thorough search, nothing showed up but an old button.

Hattie stood up and flopped down on the piano bench and gazed down at the yellowed music sheet, O Holy Night. Hattie felt a moment of the past creeping into her senses before her detective skills became alert and she stood up quickly and opened the bench, thinking Susanne could have had the key in her pocket while sitting on the hard bench and it was cutting into her leg as she played, so she removed it and put it someplace secure. The inside had serval sheets of old music, an old hymnal, and one very tiny key!

Sitting at the desk, Hattie searched around the busy pattern again until she felt the tiny keyhole and smiled. "Now, to see

94

if this little key works!" with steady fingers, Hattie inserted the small key and gave it a turn, popping the rectangle door open. Without having seen the light of day for over 200 years, the box of cards appeared brand new, although the design was dated to the 1800's. Turning the top card over, she smiled to herself and whispered. "Number 2." Looking at the other eight, she knew Avery Torrance had the first Christmas card. "Now to find the New Year's invitations." Hattie felt inside the secret mini closet and pulled out another box. It held several pieces of jewelry, and a ring of keys, a variety of sizes. Hattie noticed one large key lying alone in the bottom. She placed the jewelry back, along with the ring of keys, but kept out the larger key.

Hattie turned it around in her hand and noticed it was shiny and new. "This looks like the size of the house key William left in the entrance door when he unlocked it for me to bring the box out. Could this key have belonged to the cottage William was having built for Avery? Susanne would not have had their key inside her secret compartment or they would have tried to use it to escape, knowing they would die anyway if they remained inside." The other two secret drawers didn't need a key to open, you just had to find them in the busy pattern. The first drawer had Pattie's baby silver cup, cap, and baptism gown. Opening the second drawer, she laughed out. "Invitations! Twenty invites that never received their cards." Hattie read one and found no clues so placed them back to keep her husband from seeing them and risk getting him upset again. Hattie checked her watch when the hall clock stuck six. "Good old reliable Timex, always on time! Just like my William." She walked to the entrance hall and smiled when he drove up.

"Do you think we will be doing any time traveling tonight Hattie, my love?" William and Hattie had eaten and were strolling around the grounds at her request. "Are we looking for anything in particular out here this evening darling?"

"To answer your first question, my inquisitive husband, I haven't the slightest ideal what we might experience tonight at midnight." Hattie gave his hand a loving squeeze. "I had thought about looking over the stables and carriage house. If the Torrance's cottage is still intact, I would like to see it as well."

"Darling, all three of those are spaced pretty far apart and they are quite large inside." William never questioned his wife's request, knowing she had a good reason for wanting to see each place. "As for the cottage, I am not sure what condition it is in now, if its still intact at all. I'm sure trees and high weeds have taken it over by now"

Hattie stopped and pulled out the shiny key, handing it to her husband. "I found this key in Susanne's secret mini closet and thought it might belong to the cottage."

William turned the key over in his hand, trying to recall where he had seen it after over 200 years. "It certainly looks like an old 1800's house key. It is made of solid brass and quite heavy for a key, but so was my keys to the mansion."

"Did Susanne have a spare key, in case one was lost?" Hattie watched William looking down a grown-up path. "What was down that path darling? I don't recall seeing it before we had the grounds landscaped for the bed and breakfast."

"Now who's the inquisitive partner?" William laughed when Hattie slapped his arm playfully. "As for Susanne having a spare key to the house, no she did not. This sad old path led to Avery's family's new home, they never got to use, thanks to my selfish need to stay young." William put his arm around her, to show her he had overcome the gilt he had been carrying earlier. "There is time for one place this evening, so you may choose."

"Since the path is before us and it is winter and the snakes are in hibernation, I choose the cottage remains." Hattie happily walked along beside her handsome husband through the overgrown path that curved around for about four-tenths of a mile until they came to the ruins of a once almost finished dream home for Avery and Charlotte Torrance and their two children. Hattie was disappointed to find the walls fallen inside and the front door where she had hoped to open with the brass key, was lying face down on the frozen ground. "How terribly sad. A once beautiful dream fallen to ruin."

"I'm truly sorry Hattie, darling. Like you, I had foolish hopes we would find the cottage standing like new." William handed the key back to Hattie then turned his disappointed wife around and headed back to the mansion.

CHAPTER 18

When the clock in the lower hall struck twelve, Hattie felt a hand on her arm and opened her eyes slowly. She had fallen to sleep after making love to William and turned to find him fast asleep beside her. Pulling the sheet up around her naked body, she sat up and peered around in the dark room, thinking she had only imagined someone touching her. She reached over at the bedside table for her watch, touching the light button. It read 12:05a.m. Nothing in the room had changed, so she knew they were still in the present time. She concluded she had been dreaming, and started to nestle down next to her sleeping husband when she heard a voice near the door.

"Hattie Russel, come with me to my cottage, the one you went to see last evening before you came up to bed."

"Avery?" she started to reach for her robe she had placed in a chair by the bed. It wasn't there, the chair or the robe. She certainly could not get out of bed without her gown on and it was still in the closet. "I seem to be at a disadvantage here, Mr. Torrance." She spoke up, hoping William would wake up, but he never stirred. Hattie reached over to shake him and found the bed empty.

"He's not there Hattie." Again, the calm man's voice. "William is back in 2025."

"Then, we must be in your 1814 bedroom." Hattie suddenly realized she was dressed in a wool gown, so she climbed out of the bed and felt some sort of slippers under her feet. "Have I a robe as well, Avery? I cannot very well go outside in the cold in just a gown." Hattie felt strange talking to a complete stranger in her and William's room.

"Hattie, your and William's room is ahead, in the future. This is my room, 1814, but I am a married man and a gentleman, Mrs. Marshall." Again, the invisible man was very polite and it was obvious to Hattie he could read her mind

"There is a coat waiting for you by the door."

"Mr. Torrance, how do you know my name is Hattie Russel Marshall?" Hattie moved slowly toward the voice by the door. "If you are from the 1800's, you would have known William was married to Susanne."

"Yes, a very compassionate lady she was too." The voice sounded sad when he added. "And he had a very precious and sweet daughter, Pattie. I wanted to save them, but for some reason, I could not even save myself."

"Avery, what happened to you? What did those demons do to make everyone forget you?" Hattie reached the door and saw a wool coat floating in the air. She reached for it and was startled when she saw a man standing there, dressed in 1800's attire. "Avery Torrance?"

"Yes ma'am, I am Avery Torrance and to answer your questions, I cannot know what happen to me on that night, because it has not happened yet. I am reliving the 23rd of December this night as I have every Christmas season for over 200 years." He opened the door and motioned for her to follow him. "I will be taking you the fast way so we will be outside in a blink of an eye.

"This is the path William took me down after dinner last night, but it's not grown up anymore." Hattie walked along the lovely pathway until they came to the cottage, standing tall. "Its not fallen down anymore!"

"No, it has just been built, Hattie." Avery had tears in his eyes. "It was to be my family's home in the springtime, but as fate would have it, I never saw my Charlotte or children again." The apparition looked down at her, deep concern written on his handsome face. "Hattie, do you think my Charlotte forgot I existed too and Evan and little Fannie?"

"I can assure you Avery, Charlotte never forgot you, or your children. She saved every letter and Christmas card you sent her. I know because I have read everyone of them." Hattie wondered if he had the Christmas card on him, but would wait to see if he mentioned it first.

"Hattie, how did you get those letters I wrote my darling wife?" Avery seemed to relax and Hattie felt sure he had carried that question of their remembering him around with him all these many years and she felt glad that burden was off his shoulder.

"Your granddaughter, five greats up, brought them for me to read, hoping I could find some clues as to your whereabouts."

"Granddaughter? A grandchild from one of my children." Avery stared at the unfinished house, tears rolling down his cheeks. "I missed Evan and Fannie growing up, their weddings and having babies of their own, then growing old to see their grandchildren have children."

"I never meant to upset you Avery. Was there a purpose for your bringing me to the cottage?" Hattie wanted to change the subject for the sad spirit and it seemed to work when he looked down smiling.

"You found my key today and I have needed it for years to look inside."

"The brass key! Yes, I did find it Avery, but I can assure you it is not in the wool gown." Hattie tried to figure out why he started laughing at her statement.

"No, it wouldn't be because the key is in my hand. I retrieved it from your man pants."

"Man pants?" Hattie studied his statement for a moment before realizing woman never wore pants in the 1800's. "Well, fashions have changed in my century and the key does belong to you anyway, right?"

"Right!" Avery stuck the key in his pocket and gave her a wink.

"So, aren't you going inside?" she was trying to figure this spirit out. He had been wanting the key to go inside and now that he had it, he did not seem to want to see inside as much as she did.

"I cannot go inside this night because I did not in 1814." He patted his vest pocket. "I really hate to end our talk my dear, but I still have to finish Charlotte's letter to get off tomorrow and hopefully her special Christmas card, tucked away safely inside my vest."

"The number 1 Christmas card is inside your vest pocket?" Hattie finally knew where the carriage driver had kept the card.

"Tucked away, safe and sound!" he smiled "Sweet dreams Hattie Russel Marshall. I've got to get back to my room before my time is up and you must get back to your worried husband, who is searching franticly for his wife."

Before Hattie could say another word, Avery Torrance was gone and she was standing in front of the old cottage ruins, alone in the woods with only her robe on. "Hattie Russel, you have been in some ridiculous situations before, but this beats them all." She turned toward the path, which seem bright moments before and now with the overgrown trees and weeds, the way back was dark and dreary. As she stumbled along, Hattie thought she heard her husband's voice calling her. She paused to listen and breathed a sigh of relief when she recognized William and Andrew calling her.

"Down the path!" Hattie called out and could hear quick footsteps running her way. Noticing the flashlights, Hattie stopped and continued to call out to them until they found her, looking sheepishly. "Hi fellows! I guess you're wondering why I am walking around in the dark of night, alone in the woods."

"It did cross our minds, sis." Andrew let out a sigh of relief as William grabbed around his wife.

"Hattie, darling, I can't imagine what made you come back to that cottage in the middle of the night. Care to explain."

"It appeared I had no choice, William darling. Avery Torrance wanted me to see his cottage before it fell to ruin." Both men stared at each other, unsure what had just happened or if Hattie had been dreaming about the finished cottage and came out in her sleep.

"Sis, you have never sleepwalked before so what gives?" Andrew looked perplexed.

"At the stroke of midnight, I, was awaken by someone calling my name." Hattie looked up at her husband, concern written on his handsome face. "I looked over and found you fast asleep, so I just assumed I was dreaming and the grandfather clock had woken me up. Then I heard Avery Torrance speaking to me and he called me by my full name the second time, Hattie Russel Marshall. I felt for you, William, trying to wake you, but I was alone in the bed, Mr. Torrance's 1814 bed." She heard her husband grunt, causing her to smile. "Not to worry darling, Avery Torrance was standing by the door being a perfect gentleman."

"You saw him?" William was wondering if Hattie was still naked in his old carriage driver's bedroom. "So, you managed to get into your robe without Avery seeing you?"

Hattie laughed, giving her husband a hug. "Darling, if I were in the 1814 bedroom, my robe was still with you." She smiled when his eyebrow went up. "I had on a very scratchy wool gown and some kind of slippers when I got out of bed and the perfect gentleman had a wool coat waiting for me to wear outside. Somehow, Avery knew I had found the key to his cottage and that was the reason he took me there."

"Hattie, then you had the opportunity to ask him what happen to him so we would know where to find his body, right?" Andrew asked hopeful, before yawning.

"You know I ask him" She started walking, feeling the night air growing colder. "He couldn't tell me because he said it had not happened yet."

"What kind of answer was that? It doesn't make any sense." Andrew scratched his messy hair.

"Avery is an apparition Andrew, he is not real, only a wondering spirit, reliving the three nights before Christmas, 1814." Hattie stopped to look up at the mansion "If I have the chance to be with Avery tomorrow evening, I might know the answer."

"But Hattie, it isn't even December 22 yet, how can Avery's spirit relive what happen before the date gets here?" William had calmed down after finding his wife safe and not taken by some demons.

"I think that is one of his punishments, darling." Hattie had time to figure out the reason the carriage driver relived those three nights over and over, starting with the festival. The strange sounds only accrue when the festival begins and the seasons guest are staying in room #6 and the noises are heard in the library." She looked back at her brother. "Andrew, you know yourself that from December 25th until the following Thanksgiving-day, those rooms are as quiet as a mouse, right?"

"Yes, come to think of it." Andrew opened the door for the couple, then whispered. "So, you're saying, the demons are responsible for Avery Torrance's disappearance and have put a curse on his poor spirit to relive what happened over and over during the festival, between Thanksgiving and Christmas Eve."

"It appears to be that way Andrew." Hattie spoke softly. "There will be no more hauntings tonight, so you may get back to bed before Shannon wakes up and finds you missing. If I do not get a chance to find out tomorrow night, I have still got several more changes to find the answer, perhaps even on Christmas Eve itself." Hattie's attention went to the third floor. "And when I find Avery Torrance's body, I know where I will find the missing Christmas card."

CHAPTER 19

The town streets were crowded with festival visitors when Hattie found her daddy and grandpa at the park square, selling their produce. She had asked them to set her up a table to sell the Hattie's-Patties and William & Hattie's dance cookies, along with copies of her book, The Box in the Attic. It felt like old times being with her family at the market and brought back memories of meeting her William at the very same spot her father had sat her table.

"Hi darling, it's great to see my little girl again, selling at the market with her daddy." Grandpa Gideon gave her one of his famous hugs and a big kiss, before giving his booming laugh. "We brought you a lot of them pretty little cookies you design and had to hold the crowd back from buying them until you arrived."

"Papa is right, Hattie darling. I just bet my girl will be sold out before one o'clock." Adam Russel looked out at the gathering crowd. "I see you already have a long line of customers although I don't think anyone of them will be as exciting as your first sale, when my baby was just ten and met Mr. Marshall for the very first time."

"You're right daddy. I will never forget that special day, seeing his black boots, then his long black wool coat before standing up to look into his serious handsome face, which looked even more handsome when he smiled." Hattie gave her daddy a hug before grabbing a big red apple and giving her grandpa a wink. "Just put that on my tab, grandpa."

"You're all paid up, Hattie sweetheart. We have had four of your great cookies already for our snack this morning." He gave her a wink and nodded to the long line waiting for her. "Better run alone and start selling them cookies before your daddy and I eat them up!"

"I'll send them over to your stand for some of your homemade apple cider to wash them down with." Hattie chuckled and started selling her items. As she was about to sell her last cookies, she glanced up to see the Caswell brothers staring down at her.

"What can I do for you boys? I have a few cookies left and a couple of my books for sale." Hattie had stood up when she saw who her customers were.

"Your cookies look so…cute. Wouldn't you agree brother shorty?" the tallest brother gave her a smirk and she knew he was the outspoken one of the group when his brothers laughed at his comment.

"Look Mr. Caswell, do you or do you not want to buy anything from me?" Hattie didn't particularly like their attitude and wanted the rude men to move on. She had not noticed her husband walk up on the scene.

"You heard my wife, fellows. If you don't wish to buy anything from Mrs. Marshall then I expect you to get lost!" The young men gave him a cocky smile and walked away, through the crowd. "Hattie, how long have those jerks been bothering you?"

"Not very long, my dear protecting husband." She gave him a big smile, still feeling butterflies at the sight of him. "You're in the market early darling. I thought you might be busy with last minute orders from the mill."

"The truth is, I was busy at my office desk in the mill when I got an unusual phone call, telling me my wife could be in danger if I did not go to her at once." William looked toward the fleeting Caswell brothers and wondered what their, intentions had been concerning Hattie. "I have a hunch it had something to do with that rough group of young men."

"The Caswell's are nothing but trouble and ever since they came to Sleepy Creek to live with Harvey Caswell, their parents, Jack and Wanda Caswell haven't done anything to curve their bad actions." Hattie smiled at June and Tracy Farrell from the Sleepy Creek Café and Bakery when they walked up swiftly, wallets in their hand.

"Please tell us you have some cookies left to sale, Hattie dear." June breathed heavily after her dash across the snowy grass from their little business.

"I do have twenty-five left, Miss Farrell. A mixture of Hattie's-Patties and William and Hattie's dance. How many would you like?" Hattie reached for a handle bag to place the cookies in.

"Twenty-five? We will take all of them darling." Tracy opened her wallet after Hattie added up the sale. "I see you have two of your books left. We will take them too, right sister?"

"Oh yes sister, we never turn down a chance to get two more copies of The Box in the Attic." The friendly sisters gave Hattie double the cost and patted her head, as they did when she was ten. "Every festival you choose a different charity to give all your sale money too and this year is just as rewarding as all the others."

"Refurbish the old cemetery fund, how appropriate for a town as old as Sleepy Creek." Tracy picked up the bag of cookies and handed her sister June the books "Many of our ancestors are buried in that old graveyard and the head stones have become almost unreadable. Knowing your detective skills for tracking down things, I'm sure you can find the lost records for who goes where."

"Yes ma'am, I have already given the map with grave sites to the stone carver." Hattie felt William's hand incircle her waist.

"We can assure you ladies, one of the oldest cemeteries in North Carolina will be good as new when we are finished." William knew he had the sister's attention. "I too have done my research and find several stones date back to the 1700's, way before I came to Sleepy Creek. The old graveyard has gone far too long in decay and it is time we pay some respect to those souls buried there."

"Such a fine couple, wouldn't you agree sister?" June looked at them with admiration.

"Indeed, I do, sister." Tracy took out a tissue to blow her nose, as she sniffed back the tears. "Please come by the Café for lunch today. It is on the house." She checked her watch and grabbed her sister's arm. "I never dreamed we had stayed this long sister. The staff will be wondering what happen to us, and right here at lunch time." The Farrell sisters gave one last wave and with little fast steps they rushed to their café and bakery.

"Those brothers are out of sight now." Hattie packed up her things as William carried her small table over to the Russel fruit and vegetable stand. "I hope I don't see them until the games when my brothers beat the pants off them!"

Adam had been keeping an eye on the Caswell brothers when they walked up to harass his daughter and was ready to take matters into his own hands when he noticed William Marshall making his way swiftly across the street, before dashing passed shoppers in the market square to reach his wife. Adam felt a sense of relief to know his son-in-law cared so much for his little girl and was ready to defend her.

"Hattie, what did those Caswell boys want?" Adam took the table from William and placed it on the wagon.

"I can tell you Adam, those troublemakers weren't looking to buy her cookies!" William held her protectively. "I felt like smashing that oldest boy right in the mouth for harassing my woman!"

"My gallant darling, you would have been outnumbered had you started a fight with that rude jerk!" Hattie never felt like the damsel in distress and could pretty much take care of any circumstances on her own. But there was something about those brothers that made her blood run cold. Maybe it was their attitude, the fact that they enjoyed bullying others, especially the fairer sex or weaker men. Hattie also knew her husband lived by the 1800's standards and men from that area treated their woman like porcelain dolls and defended them whenever they were mistreated. She had no doubt, William could take on that entire Caswell family if he thought they were abusing her. Hattie glanced up to see him staring down, eyes unblinking.

"William, I know you could have taken on all three of those imbeciles on your own, but then we would have had to skip lunch at Sleepy Creek Café and Bakery to go home to the cottage for a change of clothes."

William's frown melted into a big grin as he lifted her up into his arms and kissed her. "I might have looked a mess after defending my dearest love, but those three would have passed for mud wallowing pigs after I got finished with them!"

"Maybe it's best if you leave that bunch along, my friend." Reverend Westly had walked up and heard the conversation. "I've heard many church goers tell me of unsolved crimes in Sleepy Creek since that family moved in. House break ins, checks stolen from rural mailboxes, items that have been shop lifted, just to name a few." The preacher's attention fell on Handyman Harvey's Hardware Store. "I was just on my way to the hospital to check on poor old Harvey Caswell who accidently fell down the flight of steps leading to his store."

"Jim, what was Harvey doing upstairs? He has been living on the first floor next to his store ever since his wife got sick." Gideon walked up after hearing his old friend's name mention. "It's those kinfolk of his I betcha! That nephew of his just showing up out of the blue after hearing about Bertha's death." Grandpa Gideon took his old worn wool hat off and scratched his white ruffled-up hair. "I ain't seen Harvey since he came to the farm right after they showed up, telling me how they same as took over the hardware store and told him he needed to take it easy! Baa! I say one of them no count boys done pushed my old friend down them stairs to get rid of him!"

"Pa, you don't have any proof and if Harvey is unconscious we may never know what happened." Adam felt bad for his father's old friend and prayed the dear man would come to so he could tell what happen. "Jim, how is Harvey doing? Is he going to make it?"

"There are a lot of prayers going up for Harvey, Adam, but it doesn't look good." Reverend Westly turned to Hattie who had been taking in the horrible news of the gentle old hardware handyman who had been in operation for years. "Hattie, could I get you and William, if you're not busy, to come with me to see what the doctors have to say?"

"I really need to get back to the mill, Jim, but if Hattie has time, she may assist you in finding out how Mr. Caswell is doing." William held tight to his wife's hand, feeling nervous over this new revelation. "Please tell the doctors to hold no treatments due to cost. I will cover all his medical bills." His eyes fell on Hattie. "Darling, please be careful and stick with Reverend Westly. If you make it to the café tell the sisters I had to get back to work. If you need me, do not hesitate to call, understand?"

"Yes darling. Should I get in a tight spot, I will call my knight in shining armor." With one more kiss, William reluctantly walked away.

"Hattie, I can see William Marshall is totally devoted to you." Jim Westly began walking toward his car and helped her in. "I can't help but believe your husband feels there's something unusual about those Caswell boys, same as me."

"Yes, I agree there is something there I haven't quite put my finger on, but the strange coldness I feel when they are near is much like the feelings I had around Theodore Johnson." Hattie looked over for Reverend Westly to react to her words and saw him nodding his head. "Then, you would agree they act demoniac?"

"Studying fallen angels, they easily fit their traits, but they also fit an unrulily bunch of atheists, set out to disrupt a Christian holiday." The minister of the Methodist Church drove into the hospital parking lot and climbed out, along with Hattie. "Let's hope the doctors have a good report on Mr. Caswell."

"There has been no change in the patient since his admittance two hours ago." The leading doctor over Harvey Caswell's care had laid the files out on his desk, to go over what they had learned so far. "The paramedics found the patient lying at the foot of the stairs, just as Jack Caswell, the patient's nephew, said when he called the emergency line." The doctor looked up skeptical "He claimed the older Caswell had came upstairs to bring fresh linens for the bathrooms but there were no signs of a severe fall. Not a single bone broken, only a single blow to the head, such as could be made by a hard hit on the skull."

"Doctor Parks, are you indicating Mr. Caswell was struck on his head intentionally?" Hattie knew any member of Jack Caswell's family were capable of striking Harvey across the back of his head, then drag his body to the bottom of the stairs. "That would be attempted murder! Should Harvey Caswell cease to live, then the crime will be murder."

"We cannot claim such a theory as of yet, Mrs. Marshall, until all our test is done." Doctor Parks had had the same conclusion but had to be medically correct on his findings. "Then to prove someone did the hideous act will be up to the attorneys."

"Well, let us pray the person who is responsible for this misjustice will be punished to the fullest extent of the law." Reverend James Westly stood up and helped Hattie with her coat. "Can we see Mr. Caswell?"

"I can find no reason why you cannot." Doctor Parks rang for a nurse. "Please see Reverend Westly and Mrs. Marshall to room 312 and permit them some privacy for as long as they need." The doctor had stood when Hattie rose from her seat. "Sometimes it helps a comatose patient to hear someone speak his name and say a few things. I wouldn't bet that it will work in his case, but it's worth a try."

Hattie looked down at the friendly old man who had visited the Russel farm for many years, way before she was born. She recalled sitting around listening to her grandpa and Harvey recall their youth, growing up just a mile apart. Attending the little red schoolhouse near the town, liking the same freckle-face girl with long brown pigtails, name Nettie Riggins. Now Grandpa Gideon's long-time friend lay in critical condition and might never live to remember growing up in Sleepy Creek.

"Uncle Harvey..." Hattie had called him uncle as a small girl and remembered how he would chuckle as he grabbed the giggling child, giving her a bunch of kisses. "Uncle Harvey, it's Hattie Russel! I sure do miss you and grandpa kidding one another about who caught the biggest fish in Sleepy Creek." Hattie took his hand and rubbed it as she continued. "Why, my grandma Nettie just laughed and laughed at you two and declared the biggest fish either of you had ever caught in the creek was no bigger than a tadpole." Hattie laughed remembering Grandpa Gideon and Harvey's face. "Why, I ain't every seen a beet any redder than your and Grandpa Gideon's faces! It was about the funniest thing I had ever seen and heard when grandpa admitted all he caught was a stupid tadpole and you confessed to slipping your pet goldfish from home for your catch!" Hattie stopped when she felt Harvey move his fingers under her embrace. She turned and gave Reverend Westly a hopeful smile. "Uncle Harvey, the truth of the matter was, Grandma Nettie declared catching the biggest fish, a ten-pound catfish, and she fixed it for everyone's supper!" Hattie had made up that story and hoped it would trigger his mind.

Hattie sat up when Harvey opened his eyes and declared. "That Nettie Russel did no so thing! We felt so bad about our poor catch, we up and took that woman to Sleepy Creek Fish House and fed her supper!" He gave Hattie a wink, then wrinkled his brow from the pain. "Now that's the first time my wink smarted a mite!"

Hattie rang for the nurse, as she laughed with total happiness. "Welcome back Uncle Harvey!"

"Have I been away?" he looked over Hattie's shoulder and saw his minister. "Where have I been?"

"Uncle Harvey, You, were either trying to be Sleeping Beauty or Rip Van Winkle, so which was it?" She laughed when he scratched his chin, trying to decide. "The truth is, you were hit on the head and fell unconscious. Now you are in Sleepy Creek Hospital..." the nurse ran in, eyes wide as she ran back out for the doctor. "And you have a pretty nurse to take care of you."

"Looks like that pretty nurse is scared of me." He gazed toward the door, eyes wide.

"She is just happy to see you awake and has gone to fetch your doctor." Hattie stood up when Doctor Paul walked swiftly inside. "It appears you lost the bet doctor. Uncle Harvey is back with us and can tell us what happened when he hit his head."

"Hit my head! Pooh! More like got smashed on the old noggin when I, weren't looking! I think I will stay right here, if you don't mind!" The old timer crossed his arms in deviance. "I don't see how come that nephew just showed up out of the blue when I hadn't seen the little scant since he was two years old. I was doing just find on my own, mind you."

"Mr. Caswell, we can keep you until we feel it's safe to release you from the hospital, but after that, you have to return to your home or find a friend to take you in." Doctor Paul could not get over the man's quick recovery."

"Go home to those misfits! I just as soon stayed asleep right here!"

"Uncle Harvey, you do not have to go back into your house until we find a reason to run your so-called misfit family out. I am more than positive your old friend Gideon would agree and find room for you at the farm."

"Then its settled! Hattie, you were always a smart young'un." Harvey Caswell relaxed. "Tell my old friend, he can come fetch me as soon as old doc here gives me the boot!"

Hattie chuckled when the doctor tried to hide his smile, then she leaned over and gave Harvey a kiss on his forehead. "Behave yourself Uncle Harvey and don't worry about your unwanted guest. I have a hunch they will be gone before Christmas comes!"

Hattie sat quietly, her mind in full gallop, when Reverend Westly pulled back into town square. "You have been mighty quiet since we left the hospital. What's going through that sharp head of yours, Hattie?"

"Harvey hasn't seen his nephew since he was two-years-old, so maybe this Jack Caswell is not who he says he is." Hattie knew she had her minister's attention. "I believe this family, if they really are a family, have come to Sleepy Creek on a mission or perhaps...they have always been close by and only until recently became visible to protect something they are hiding."

"Hiding? Like what Hattie?" Jim Westly looked confused.

"Not what Jim, who. I believe they are afraid I am getting too close to finding Avery Torrance!"

CHAPTER 20

Hattie and William had found the rest of the Russel family seated by the round skating rink watching the Russel boys warming up with the Brower brothers. They had joined forces to defeat the rowdy Caswell clan, across the rink staring at their opponents with cocky grins. Hattie looked over at their disordered faces and narrowed her eyes at them.

"I hope the Russel's and Brower's whip those rude devil's butts!" she did not blink when the oldest brother saw her watching and took off his toboggan and swept it in front of him as he gave a bow. All Hattie's brothers had saw what had happened and walked over to their sister, stopping in front of her.

"Hattie, we didn't like the way that creep was looking at you." Andrew glanced back to see him still looking their way. "There is something weird about that group." He looked down at William who also had been observing from his seat. "William, it may be wise to keep close to our sister as long as those Caswell's are still around."

"If we can prove Harvey's so-call fall wasn't an accident, they might be leaving sooner than you think!" Grandpa Gideon had just returned from visiting his old friend at the hospital and had heard his side of the story. "I think that nephew is out to get everything Harvey has and those no count sons of Jacks are just mean enough to hit an old man on his head in hopes of killing him, then pretending my old friend took a spill down those steps!"

"I couldn't disagree with you more grandpa!" Matthew rubbed his left arm, remembering the pain he had felt at the last years games when the one they refer to as tank, slid into him on the slops running him into a tree. He gave a chuckle remembering competing with the Brower's before they became friends. "This bunch of hoodlums made you Brower's look pretty good when we competed in the games while still enemies." Matthew looked over at the Caswell's. "I would not doubt they would try to murder their competitor just to win!"

"Hattie, what is your take on the Caswell brothers?" Adam had been listening to all the distrust for this new family that had moved in with Harvey Caswell last year, just before the festival began. "Papa thinks they had something to do with Harvey's accident and your brothers don't trust them, especially during the games."

"And my brothers, as well as the Brower's boys, are right not to trust those three young men, nor their so-called parents." Hattie knew she had everyone's attention. "Boys, I think you must watch your back as well as your teammate's back, during every game. I've asked William to have spotters on the slops this year and camera's set up to view the entire downhill sled run. All the spectators can watch on a big screen that will lower before the sled run game begins. My darling husband thought of that and has hired a technician to handle all the details." Hattie cast an eye on the opposing team. "The Caswell's have no knowledge of any of the new additions, so whatever they have planned to do to stop you will come to a halt." Hattie looked over at her parents and grandparents who had been listening to their intelligent daughter.

"Grandpa, I also believe that one of those Caswell men tried to kill Harvey and make it look like an accident. I also believe their name is not Caswell at all and they have been known to go by a variety of other names, including..." Hattie reached for her husband's hand and looked him in the eye. "Theodore Johnson and Clarence Rockford."

"Hattie darling, are you saying those Caswell's are not human but demons disguising as people?" William bounced his baby girl in his lap as she giggled at the happy children chasing each other in a pretend winter game, unaware of the danger around them. "Can you be certain these people are demons and not just a bunch of bullies, out to frighten good Christian people?"

"William, I cannot prove anything right now, but that is my theory. Until I can find the real Jack Caswell, if he is still alive, I cannot bring my findings out in the open." Hattie stopped when the announcer called for the skaters to get into position. She, lend over to whisper into her husband's ear when everyone sat up to watch the first game. "If what I think is correct, the demons that hid Avery are on to our remembrance of him and know that we are getting close in finding him. Even if the law authority, find them suspicious of attempted murder, they could never contain them in a cell or bring them to justice. It could prove dangerous to everyone living in Sleepy Creek if we let on that we are on to them."

"So, the authorities should be warned to back off until we can prove your theory, my love." William watched the skaters race around the rink and it was obvious the so-called Caswell's had an unnatural speed. "I am beginning to see what you mean darling. No human can skate that fast for that length of time. I have lived the hell a demon can place you in and unless something is done to slow that bunch up, our team won't stand a chance to win either game."

"I think I know what will distract the leader. The other two will fade back if he slows up." Hattie stood up, staring out at the tall 'Caswell'. William grabbed her hand.

"Hattie, what are you planning? I do not want you to risk your life over these games! They're not worth you getting in danger with that demon!"

"I will be perfectly safe, William." Hattie smiled and nodded her head toward the large carriage, hooked up with the four white horses. "I will simply ask Benson to take me on a little night ride, around the big rink."

"Oh, I see what you're up to, my clever girl." William kissed her when she bent down smiling. "You are thinking when they see the carriage moving by with you sitting with the driver, the demons will think you are with Avery Torrance instead of Benson, who is dressed in 1800's attire."

"Wish me luck!"

"I have a hunch you will not need luck, Mrs. Marshall."
William pointed at the moonlight dancing along the path
around the big pond. "A perfect night for a ghostly ride."

"Benson, keep the horses moving at a slow trot, making it
look like we're floating." Hattie had convinced their present
carriage driver to take her around the frozen lake.

"Madam, this is most unusual." The driver started the
horses in a slow trot, like she asked. "Hattie, you aren't trying
to distract the opposing team, are you? Not that I blame you.
It's obvious they can beat any skater on earth with their speed."

"Well, actually Benson, that is exactly what I am doing."
Hattie felt the driver watching her but she was watching the tall
Caswell who had obviously spotted the carriage and slowed up,
keeping his attention on the carriage while Andrew and his
team mates flew passed the confused Caswell's. "And my plan
worked. This is one game those cheaters will not steal from the
real champions."

Hattie was rubbing the horse's head talking to Benson
when the tall leader walked up. "Mr. Caswell, how did the
game end?" Hattie smiled, knowing her brother's team had
won. "I couldn't tell who was leading on the carriage. My
husband has set spotters all round to make sure each game is
played fairly. I volunteered for the spotter around the frozen
pond and thought the best way to make it around was by
carriage. You were ahead on turn seven, my place to spot."

"We lost! I was curious about the sudden appearance of the
old carriage." Travis Caswell stared at the period dressed
driver. "I was distracted momentarily but I will be on guard at
the next game for a spotter and we shall come out the winner
after winning the next two games."

"Well then, I must warn you sir, the hill will be well lit and
spotters will be stationed at every turn." Hattie would leave out
the camera's and screen viewing below for spectators. "Any
sign of cheating from either team will mean automatic
dismissal from the games!" Hattie walked away beside of their
driver, leaving the 'tall' brother fuming.

Knowing they could not play any tricks on the opposing side, the Caswell brothers knew their unusual powers could get them down the long snowy hill with lighting speed, so the score was tied up. Hattie paced around behind William and her family, trying to come up with a way for the Russel's and Brower's to win back the title of festival champions. She had not participated in the festival games ever since William returned, but being a Russel, she could join in if she could come up with something to distract the Caswell's again. Hattie was about to give up when Mr. Edwards walked over and offered his services.'"

"Hattie, I use to be the champion rope puller on my high-school team and we won ever tug of war, no matter the time of year. I was from Mt. Mitchell and it doesn't get any colder than there in North Carolina."

"Let me see if the judges will accept you as a member of the Russel-Brower team." Hattie knew their driver had strong muscles because she had witness him lifting up the carriage on a big block to change the wheels for sleds. William had been listening and motioned for the head judge to come over.

"Yes sir, Mr. Marshall and what can I do for you sir?" The score pad shook in his hand getting called over by the man who own practically the entire town. "I had to give the Caswell the sled win, sir. They flew right past both Russel's and Bart Brower."

"Flew would be an appropriate word, Mr. Jackson, but that is not why I called you over." William motioned for Hattie and his driver to step up next to him. "For some strange reason, these Caswell's have the power to win any game and the average person, no matter how athletic they are, don't stand a chance."

"I couldn't agree more Mr. Marshall, but what can I do? If they come in first and win, even if it seems unfair, there's, nothing the judges can do but declare them the winners."

"My family does not stand a chance in the rope pull when their opponents have unnatural strength, would you not agree?"

William looked across the ice to see the brothers looking their way and laughing, sure of their victory. "We are not bowing out of the games, Frank, we are just asking for a replacement on our team. I wrote the rules Frank, now I am changing them. We want to switch our weakest player with Benson Edwards."

CHAPTER 21

Hattie and William walked up the stairs to room #6, laughing about the last game and how their driver seem to take the Caswell's by surprise as he easily pulled them in the icy water, almost single handedly.

"I have never witness anything quite as funny as seeing those cocky brothers fall in the big hole chopped out on the frozen pond!" Hattie knew her laughter would not disturb the other guest due to the fact, the entire occupants of Marshall Mansion Inn had been driven in for the night games, a festival favorite.

"There was a tense moment for a time when the rope slid back and forth until our clever driver suddenly surprised them with one quick jerk, sending the bragging bullies in the ice-cold water." William stopped as he recalled their appearance when they finally came up out of the water. "Did you see their faces when they rose up from the cold water? They appeared to be disfigured, irregular in appearance."

"They did appear a little weird looking for a moment, but it faded pretty quickly back to the three rude young men, when they crawled out grumbling for losing to ordinary men." Hattie and William passed a few of the B&B's guest, wishing them a restful night as they turned to go to the end room. Hattie smiled as she watched her handsome husband slip into his pajamas and climb under the covers, trying to cover his yawn. Knowing William had a very busy day before coming to the games with her, Hattie climbed in her high-neck gown instead of sleeping in her birthday suit as she did almost every night since they've been married. By the time she had finished in the bathroom, her tired husband had drifted off to sleep. She crawled in next to him and even in his sleep, the charming man pulled her up close to him, never waking up.

"Hattie Russel Marshall, are you going to sleep through my visit?" Hattie felt like she had just closed her eyes, exhausted herself from the day's events, when a man's voice woke her. She glanced beside her to see if William had wakened with passion on his mind. Hattie bolted straight up and stared down at the empty spot beside her, then once again the man's voice came, over by the window. "I hated to wake you up Hattie. You were sleeping so peacefully, but you are in my room…" she thought she caught a soft laugh as he continued. "and in my bed."

"Your room? Your bed?" Hattie jumped from the covers and felt around for her bedroom slippers and robe only to feel an empty chair, before realizing she was back in 1814. "Avery Torrance, I suppose you are reliving your last Christmas Eve."

"My last Christmas Eve, hardly. I have relived what happened over and over and each time its as though I'm living it for the first time. I simply cannot remember what is going to happen until it does." Avery lit the candle on the stand next to him and smiled over at Hattie. I suppose you are wondering why you are the only one who can return to 1814."

"It has crossed my mind why I end up in your 1814 bedroom instead of both me and William, since we both go to sleep in room #6." Hattie glanced down and saw the same slippers she had worn the previous night just under the single bed and pulled them out. "Avery, is there a purpose why I come back alone?"

"There is Hattie. On my December 22nd ritual, when I go to the library and wait for Mrs. Marshall, you where in there, sitting in my chair. I spirited right through you and waited for Susanne. I was startled again to hear the conversation between Mr. Marshall…oh yes, your husband now, that came as quite a shock," Avery cleared his throat, going back to his listening to the owner of the mansion and the butler arguing. "Well, like I was saying, William Marshall and Clarence Rockford, the butler. As usual Susanne Marshall comes in, says a few pleasant exchanges, then goes over to her desk, where I follow. Only this last time, you also got up and walked over and I followed your eyes as the first Mrs. Marshall opened her desk drawer and got out some new stationary for me, along with some stamps. I knew you couldn't see us or the drawer opening, but I could tell you knew it was the middle drawer nearest you. I watched your head spring up at the sound of Susanne unlocking her secret door where she got out a beautiful box of Christmas cards and graciously gave me one to send my Charlotte." Avery turned to looked out into the garden below. "I wonder if I got it off in time. I know how much she loved the Christmas cards I sent her."

"Avery, Charlotte received the last letter you wrote her but she never got her beautiful card." Hattie couldn't help but feel sorry for the loving man, and knowing he still faced whatever hell Clarence Rockford had in store for him, was still ahead on this very day he was reliving."

"Maybe if I give the Christmas card to you Hattie." Avery turned around hopeful. "You seem to know my Charlotte, so maybe you could see that she gets it."

"Avery, I am from 2025." Hattie did not want to spell out the fact that his Charlotte was long gone. "I cannot possibly give it to her, but I can give it to your granddaughter, if its even possible for me to take it from your time to mine."

"You are right, Hattie Russel Marshall! I keep forgetting you are not a part of my present time." The hopeful look faded from his handsome face. "You will return to your time in your own clothes, not the 1814 gown so you could never take the card with you. It must remain with me."

"May I see it Avery, then I could describe it to your granddaughter, Emily, who is waiting in Sleepy Creek, back in my time" Hattie walked over as he took it out of his vest pocket and handed it over. She smiled down at the couple on the front, knocking on a green door, with the message, A Merry Christmas to You. Opening the card, she noticed the owners of the big mansion welcoming their guest, along with a friendly dog. The door was very familiar and she knew it was a special card made just for the Marshalls. Hattie handed the card back to its owner, giving him a big smile. "The card is perfect for your Charlotte, Avery. It's like the Marshall's are welcoming her into their family of friends."

"That is what I saw as well. The perfect card." Avery placed it back into his vest pocket. "When you find me Hattie Russel Marshall, then you will find the card where I just placed it and give it to my granddaughter Emily. Charlotte has no need of Christmas cards in heaven." A tear ran down his cheek. "I pray I can be with her someday soon. Please Hattie, don't give up! Do not stop hunting for me. I am close by. I just cannot remember where!"

"I will not stop searching for you Avery until I find you and I feel my time is limited to the festival. Your appearance comes from Thanksgiving night until the 24th of December, then you lay dormant for the remainder of the year." Hattie gazed at the flesh and bone man standing in front of her, ponding the reason others from the past could be heard and even seen by herself, like Susanne in the library and her darling William in the rose garden from 1814. Had he seen her standing at the window looking down on December 22nd would he have known who she was or would she have been just a stranger in his home. "I suppose to those who cannot see you, one might assume you are a ghost, same as Susanne walking into the library and moving to the desk. The fact that Susanne went to heaven in 2014 makes it impossible for her to be a ghost and a spirit does not have flesh and bones like you do Avery. My guess is those demons put a curse on you causing you to return back to 1814 and relive those last three days over and over and then you return to your resting place." Hattie knew this conversation was not a part of his December 24th day but the man was desperate to be released from this devilish curse. "On Christmas Eve 2014, when Jesus came for those trapped souls in the old mansion, you were nowhere inside and at that time, the demons had blocked our memory of you. I assume you must have been someplace outside the mansion, even away from the estate all together." Hattie took his hand. "Avery, can you remember anything about that night, when I brought the box from the attic and Susanne, Pattie, and the rest of the staff were finally set free?"

"For some reason, that night my routine changed and I found myself inside the carriage house staring out as I did every December 24th, waiting for Mr. Marshall to leave after loading up the big carriage with luggage. Instead of seeing my employer come out, I saw him standing on the front porch, pacing nervously. I heard you call his name and he rushed over to unlock the door and took the box, throwing it hard into the side garden." Avery's eyes grew wide as he recalled the grotesque monster that came from the box and began crawling toward the scared group. "I was frozen as I watched in horror the demon monster moving in, ready to devour and destroy all of you. Then I witnessed for myself your bravery, even as a ten-year-old girl. I saw the Lord appear and collect the ones trapped inside the mansion. I felt left behind as I witnessed the Son of God receive all those people I loved and been able to see every Christmas season, even though they never saw me. Even my dear friend, Lucas, seem to be ignoring my presents whenever I was inside the mansion before he was taken up with the Lord." Tears filled his eyes as he recalled the Lord looking at him standing in the carriage house. "My tongue seemed to be frozen to the top of my mouth as I wanted desperately to call out for Him to take me home to heaven too. Then I heard Jesus speak to me in spirit.

"Avery, my brother, I know you seek to come with me but until your life is over and you are freed from the hand of Lucifer, I cannot take you up." Jesus spoke with love and passion. "Hattie, my gifted child, whose faith and love is pure and strong will be the one you seek out to find you and free you from the devil's curse. She will learn the truth and the words you wrote will come to pass. Christmas is a time for miracles and hope blooms in the spring."

"Then it was heaven's plan that I find you Avery. This mystery keeps getting more and more complicated. In 2014 Jesus said, until your life is over and yet here we are in 1814. Was the Lord referring to your continuing life in the past? "

CHAPTER 22

"Emily, I didn't see you at the festival games last night. When I ask grandma why you hadn't come, she said you weren't feeling well." Hattie had paid the farm a visit to pick up her daughter for the day so Nettie could do some Christmas shopping. "I was hoping you might enjoy some of the festival while you wait on news of your granddad. You could go shopping with grandma or tag along with me today, if you like. William will be tied up at the mill all day. It gets a lot busier as Christmas grows nearer."

"I think I should like to spend some time with you Hattie." Emily smiled shyly. "I am with Nettie all day and I rarely get to see you and hear what you have found out so far."

"Then grab your coat and bag and wait in my car. I will inform grandma of your plans and be right out." Hattie walked up the familiar stairs and called to her grandmother. "Grandma, Emily will be coming with me and Mattie today. I think she is anxious to learn something about her grandfather."

"I hope that is all she wants." Nettie came out dressed for town. "The girl said she wasn't in the mood to go watch the games in the night. I think Emily is afraid of the dark, at least that is how it appears. She sleeps with a lamp on beside her bed every night and I have heard her lock the bedroom door, even after I told her no one would bother her privacy."

"Emily is a stranger in a strange town grandma. I think she's just nervous about her grandfather's disappearance and everyone in Sleepy Creek not remembering him for over 200 years." Hattie suddenly remembered her Aunt Hattie's diary and wondered why she had not written down her conversation with Mr. Torrance when she promised him she would. As she pondered the thought, Nettie could tell something was going through her granddaughter's mind.

"You have remembered something about this case, haven't you, my clever Hattie?"

"When I return to the cottage, I need to check out Aunt Hattie's diary again. I think perhaps I am missing something Hattie wrote the day she paid William a visit with her friend, Pattie and Avery took her home." Hattie gave Nettie a wink. "I may be wrong grandma, but I have a hunch that missing part is in that diary, well hidden, by the power of a fallen angel."

"Hattie darling, we read that diary together, word for word and there was no mention of a conversation with the carriage driver." Nettie put on her heavy wool coat, before grabbing her scarf and bag. "It's not just magically going to appear."

"No, it won't magically appear because its well-hidden, but I think I might know a couple of places it can be found." Hattie had promised her grandmother a lift to town and she would be riding back with her husband Gideon and Adam, Hattie's daddy. "I will let you know what I find, if it is indeed there."

Hattie had promised Emily she would take her out to show her the mansion and carriage house where her grandfather was last seen, but first she wanted to research the diary. Leaving Emily in the living room with Mattie and her nannie, Hattie closed herself inside her home office to read Aunt Hattie's entry on December 23rd, 1814.

Finding the entry, telling about her time with Pattie and ending with Mr. Marshall walking her over to the door where Avery Torrance waited to take her by the mansion before taking her back to the Russel farm. Ruling out her first ideal that the words had been erased, so a led pencil could pull them back up, Hattie saw there was not enough room left for any more writing and the next page was a new day. She lifted up the next page and felt the paper, checking for thickness. Then she checked a few other pages, and a broad smile fell on her beautiful face as she wet her fingertips and pressed the page until it separated with the words: December 23rd 1814.

"Extra addition: My conversation with my friend Mr. Torrance. Dear diary, after I left my friend Pattie with her father, I felt real, bad, afraid I might never see my best friend again. As we rode along, Avery and I started talking and comparing the things we had witnessed about what was happening. He too feels something is going on with Mr. Marshall and is worried about the safety of not only Pattie but Susanne and the entire staff. The thing he witnessed in the rose garden at midnight last night while I lay sleeping peacefully next to my dearest friend, gave me the willies. Just like Pattie had confessed to telling me earlier about seeing her daddy in the rose garden speaking to something invisible, he had witnessed the same thing, except for the fact Mr. Rockford, the butler appeared in front of him. Avery had overheard a conversation earlier that evening while he waited for Susanne in the library. William Marshall and Clarence Rockford were in a heated conversation and the mean butler same as ordered his employer to be out in the garden at midnight to make some kind of bargain with something powerful and he could not change his mind once made.

Diary, Mr. Torrance's next statement really scared me when he said the butler stopped talking and his head moved slowly around and up, to stare at him through his dark window, where he thought he was well hidden. It gets more frightening. Both the butler and the invisible thing had red eyes as they stared up at Mr. Torrance. He also told me about the gruesome butler being in two places at the same time. He saw him in the town's street while waiting for the crowd to disperse and Pattie's personal maid said he had been at the mansion all day giving orders to everyone. I informed the friendly carriage driver to make it three appearances at the same time, for when Pattie and I arrived at the stone office, Mr. Rockford opened the door for us and stayed until he heard the carriage horses walk up to the entrance.

Avery promised to keep watch over Pattie and that made me feel real, good until I remembered those evil beings looking up at him and then I started worrying about his safety. With the snide remarks Rockford made to him and the warnings not to get too noisy, I'm sure all three Rockford's are watching Avery Torrance. I fear something bad is going to happen to my new friend and it nearly breaks my heart that both Pattie and Avery are in danger and I feel helpless in helping either of them without proof. I am writing these things down as a witness and if, anything every happens to Avery Torrance, maybe these words can help find out what happened to him. Hattie Russel."

"Three Rockfords?" Hattie walked over to the window and gazed out, her mind racing. "Three Caswell brothers, who look almost the same, except Travis is tall, Tank is big, and Shorty is, well short! Could their mean spirit just be a coincident? What makes them super powerful in skating, sledding, rope pulling and what cause them to get distracted again and let Mr. Edwards pull them in the water? Yes, Benson is a strong man, but that's all he is, a mortal man. These three Caswell's are not normal and could never be just mortal men." Hattie's thoughts where interrupted when Emily walked in and stopped her train of thoughts. "Are you getting anxious to visit the mansion on the hill, Emily?"

"It has been a place I have dreamed of visiting for some time Hattie." She cast her eyes down shyly. "I never meant to barge in on you, it's just that I have traveled so far to find out the truth about my grandfather Avery, and I still do not know much more than I did when I hired you."

"Emily, this is no ordinary case I have taken on. The man we are seeking has been gone for over 200 years and there are demons involved, which makes the case similar to the one I uncovered in 2014. I am on the tip of the answer and in time it will be made clearly to me. I must admit your grandfather has been a big help in bringing to light many unsolved questions."

"Hattie, I am totally confused." Emily flopped down on an easy chair. "How could my grandfather possibly help you? He has been dead for a very long time?"

"The correct word I would have chosen would be, lost or hidden." Hattie threw her pocketbook over her shoulder and motioned to the open door. "The spirit I visit in 1814 is very much alive."

"I wish I might get a visit from my devoted grandfather." Emily looked hopeful as Hattie sadly shook her head.

"I would not hold up any hopes in that happening Emily. Avery has sought me out for help, much like yourself and he chooses to see me." Hattie led her client out to her car after giving the Nannie instructions for Mattie's lunch and nap. "I will take you to the mansion and show you around. Most things are a lot different now than they were in 1814 with a few exceptions. The library has never changed, right down to the placement of Susanne's desk in the corner. The servant steps that led to the third floor have been conveniently hidden, for the B&B guest safety. The old carriage house and stables are pretty much as they were but kept up to store both carriages and horses today."

"What about my grandparent's cottage? Is it still intact or has it been neglected?" Emily stared up at the large mansion just ahead and could see the wealth behind the Marshall family that had built Sleepy Creek.

"I regret there is not much left of the former cottage, just down that overgrown path, but if you are in for a walk, I will be happy to show you its remains." Hattie pulled her car up to the front and got out pointing. "The carriage house and stables are just down that sand rock lane. I'm sure they may be of interest to you. Your grandfather spent a good deal of his time there."

"Yes, those are the places I would wish to see." Emily looked down the overgrown path, mostly an assortment of trees, most likely planted by birds or squirrels and lots of tall weeds, now brown from the winter freeze. "Maybe I can feel a little bit of my devoted grandfather Avery inside those places he spent the last years of his life at."

Hattie led her down the path she had walked through twice before. Once with her beloved William to see the sad old cottage in ruins and the second time with Avery Torrance himself, when the cottage was almost finished and stood proudly, just waiting for the Torrance family to move into.

When they stopped in front of the broken-down door and gazed inside at what once was beautiful new walls and floors, Hattie could easily recall its grandeur, standing next to Avery and hoping he would choose to go inside. She watched Avery's granddaughter walked carefully up to gaze inside, sadness written on her pretty face.

"Charlotte would have been so happy here with her beloved Avery." Tears filled Emily's blue eyes. "Stories past down concerning Grandmother Charlotte were loaded with her deep love and devotion to her husband. Those years they spent apart were very hard on her and those who remembered those years, had written down her unhappiness over their separation and if it had not been for their children, she might not have survived. Word was when she got his last troubling letter, Charlotte had the uncanny feeling that her beloved Avery would not make it to Christmas. When her promised Christmas card never came, they say the sad woman dressed in black mourning clothes for the remainder of her short life. All those who loved the good Christian wife and mother, could do nothing but stand back and watch her wither away, eternal sadness tearing up her happiness and heart."

"Emily, the poor woman had a sad and troubling life. I know the depth of complete sadness she felt after watching my own beloved William taken away from me and thinking I would never see him ever again on this earth." Hattie had hoped Avery's ghost had not heard the tragic story about the woman he devoted his life to and how she suffered his lost until the end of her life. "Avery and Charlotte's love is very simpler to mine and Williams, deep with emotions and powerful beyond almost any other kind of love. It is a love that is rooted by faith and personally blessed and handed out by the Lord Himself." Hattie turned Emily around to face her. "We must guard our words while we are near those places Avery's spirit may be resting. He might be capable of hearing what we say. The poor man has enough to deal with at the present and the past 1814 and hearing about his Charlotte's complete heartbreak and dying so young, could upset him even more."

Emily slowly backed away as she looked all around her nervously. "So, Grandfather Avery's spirit could be wondering around any one of his old hangouts?"

"Avery's spirit seems to know a lot about my life and the only way for that to be possible is to be around me when I am near his hiding place." Hattie could recall handing him the brass key and his happy smile when he placed it in his pocket. "This is one place your grandfather Avery brought me, only it was 1814 and the cottage was new, the path was trimmed with rose bushes, not a weed in sight."

"He was right here?" Emily took a deep breath, glancing back as Hattie led her back down the overgrown path toward the sand rock lane and to the carriage house, where the big carriage took up a big portion of the room.

"Our driver takes the B&B guest to Sleepy Creek for festival shopping and activities. Everything in our small town relates to the 1800's style so the guest can feel apart of the past when they take the big carriage. This is the very same carriage your grandfather drove for William and his family in the 1800's."

Emily made her way to the carriage and ran her hand lovingly over the driver's side, grabbed the rail and like an old pro, climbed up in the driver's seat. "If you're listening Avery, I am here, on your carriage waiting to hear from you and see you again."

"Emily, besides knowing your way around a carriage, just when did you hear and see your grandfather?" Hattie stood down by the driver's side looking up at the solemn face of Emily Torrance.

Emily smiled and climbed back down from the high platform. "I have heard my grandfather in my dreams many times after seeing a painting of his portrait hidden in granny Charlotte's attic. He was an amazing handsome man and granny Charlotte, as everyone called her, was the smitten image of me, or better said, I am the smitten image of granny

Charlotte, so my middle name is Charlotte." She ran her hand down the smooth carriage. "I am familiar with carriages because my own father, Frank Torrance, from Evan's line, runs a carriage service in Charleston, South Carolina, where I am one of his drivers."

"Then the Torrance tradition continues after all these years." Hattie walked over to the open-door Avery had stood and watched William bring out all his luggage, containing everything he had to get out of the mansion. She could see the side entrance to the manor house very plainly from the carriage house door and knew the driver could not have been seen watching his trusted employer's strange behavior. Hattie had blocked out the fact Emily was there walking around the large room, perhaps looking for a hiding place where her grandfather could have been put. Hattie was deep in thought." Just what happened here when William came out of the house after dinner, pretending to leave for the office and promising, no less, to come home in time to collect his family and take them to Christmas Eve services at church. That is what William had told Hattie earlier. How it happened that horrible night, when he finally bought her to see the carriage house and stables before heading to work.

Hattie hated to keep bringing up all the bad memories to her devoted husband but she knew she must get to the bottom of where the reliable carriage driver was hidden before time ran out. Friday, December 23rd would be the night of the Christmas dance and that left Christmas Eve, the night Avery Torrance disappeared. It was already Wednesday, leaving her only three days to solve the very complicated mystery. She turned to see Emily looking for perhaps some secret door and shook her head, knowing she had gone over every inch of the large carriage house and found no place large enough to conceal a full-grown man as tall as Avery Torrance. The stables would not reveal any hidden places either. If the library, servant's old stairs or the remnants of the music room did not conceal his lost body, as Hattie had crossed out due to the Lord not calling his soul out, then where could his remains be hidden? Hattie knew they had to be somewhere nearby because his ghost frequents every part of the Marshall Mansion's estate. "The only place I haven't searched is the old cottage ruins. Could Avery's body be hidden in there someplace?" Hattie knew it was time to ask her husband a few more questions which may help her uncover the carriage driver's whereabouts. She would know when she found him because he would have the missing Christmas card on him, as he had promised her.

CHAPTER 23

Hattie and Emily made their way through the rooms inside the Marshall mansion that Avery Torrance had used the most. After seeing the inside and visiting a while with Andrew and Shannon, they went out the front door. The large carriage set out front waiting for some guest who wanted a trip to Sleepy Creek on the carriage. The four white horses stood proudly for Benson Edwards as he caressed each head, calling them by name. He smiled and gave a gentleman's bow to the beautiful young women as they approached him.

"Hattie, I see you are showing Miss Torrance around. Are you planning a stay here, Miss Torrance?"

Hattie looked from her driver to her client before asking the obvious question. "How do you know one another Benson? I am certain you were not around the day she came to my office, nor later when Matthew escorted her to the farm."

"I had the pleasure of meeting this, charming young women in town last week, while I sat waiting for the group I was to bring back to the mansion." Benson had removed his hat out of respect whenever a lady was in his presence. "It appears Miss Torrance enjoys the same occupation as I."

"I was thrilled to see the beautiful carriage hooked up with such fine animals and Mr. Edwards sitting high in the driver's seat, dressed a great deal the way I dress while giving tours in Charleston." Emily gave him a shy grin. "It just reminded me of home and I felt compelled to walk over and introduce myself. I have never met a carriage driver who wasn't friendly and polite."

"And don't forget helpful." Benson teased.

"Very helpful, thank you. I asked for directions and he offered to take me, even though it wasn't but a few blocks away." Her hand automatically rubbed the horse's neck beside her. "Not wishing to interfere with his work or delaying the trip back for his riders, I graciously decided to walk."

"I guess it just came as a surprise, since I was under the impression by Grandma that you rarely left your room, except to eat meals and interact with the family a short while after dinner." Hattie gave them both a smile before adding. "I am just glad you are taking in some of the holiday festivities. I cannot wait to hear what all you did and how you managed to get passed my sharp-eyed grandma."

"It makes sense darling why Miss Torrance would be drawn to the carriage with four stately white stallions attached in front." Hattie had told William about her client Emily and Benson Edwards meeting in town. "They both drive carriages for a living, so it is a natural attraction. I am certain with their age difference, there is no physical attraction there."

"Certain are you, Mr. Marshall? The 240-year-old man who fell in love with a 10-year-old girl!" Hattie snuggled up in his arms as he chuckled at how ridiculous the truth had been.

"My girl is right, as usual. The blessing that the Lord knew how much we loved one another and let me return after you had grown into a beautiful woman was our dream come true. Much like the picture you drew of us in the future when you were only a child. Remember my Christmas gift?"

"The same picture that hangs over the mantle in our sitting room." Hattie reached up for a kiss, then smiled down at their daughter's chocolate upper lip. "Our little pumpkin loves hot chocolate with marshmallows just like her mama, don't you pretty girl?"

"Puffy fluffy snowballs! Mumm! Yummy ma-ma!" Mattie giggled and put her sippy cup to her lips for another drink and gave a big smack. William and Hattie laughed as they watched their precious daughter, advanced in her speech at four-months-old. The cute as a doll baby girl, held up a cookie crumb toward her father, blinking her big brown eyes. "Bite da-da?"

William bent down at the baby seat and pretended to take a

big bite, causing little Mattie to giggle. "Mumm, Mattie, that is almost as good as mama's Hattie's-Patties."

"Almost as good?" Hattie laughed and cleaned her daughter's mouth and lifted her from the baby seat. "That use to be a Hattie's-Patties until I crumbled it up for daddy's little girl." Hattie kissed her chubby cheek then placed her in her husband's arms. "I will get Mattie's things and we can be off to continue our conversation we were having before our charming daughter drew our attention."

Hattie and William had chosen the back, dining table at the Inn for privacy and were happily having their wine while waiting on the steak dinner. "What I cannot understand is why Emily slipped from the farmhouse without telling grandmother she was going to town."

"Maybe the girl just wanted some time to herself, darling and was afraid Nettie might ask to join her." William had learned the habits of all the Russel family since his return. Adam and Gideon preferred the fields or working with the barnyard animals. Farming was in their blood and only a couple of Hattie's brothers took to the art of farming. Carolyn left with the sons that preferred working at the cookie factory and when playboy Matthew wasn't helping Hattie, he preferred doing small jobs in town, leaving Nettie at home, by herself. It was obvious when he and Hattie visited that she was wound up with non-stop stories so Miss Torrance probably had never been around someone shut in for long periods of time with no one to talk to. "I love your grandmother dearly, darling, but you know how she can go on and on."

"Alright, that makes sense I guess." Hattie smiled at her friend Amy Collins who had got a job waiting tables in the Marshall dining room. "Thank you, Amy. This looks wonderful."

"It, taste as wonderful as it looks, Hattie. Bobby has become an excellent chef since his tour in the army's mess core." Amy refilled the glasses with wine and left them to talk.

"William, I have been thinking about all the drivers you

must have went through during your two-hundred-years being forty." She looked over to see him studying her question. "Can you remember how many different drivers you had or their names?"

"I must go back to the night I left Sleepy Creek." William took a sip of the rich red wine before speaking. "I did not leave town after I saw your Aunt Hattie in Pattie's Christmas dress and thought she had escaped the house by some miracle."

"Aunt Hattie did say after you accused her of stealing the dress, you got on the carriage and drove away like a mad man." Hattie reached for his hand. "Where did you go that night darling?"

"The mill had closed down for the holidays so I went up there and paced the floors all night, crying and swearing I would find a way to get my family and the staff out of that house!" William absent mindedly cut through his steak and took a bite as he remembered back to 1814. "I tried again a year later to get the demon in the attic to release them and he could have me. He would not hear of it and said my bargain was sealed. After seeing Hattie watching, I knew I could never return. I left Sleepy Creek, but I did not leave alone."

"Rockford! Who later changed his name to Theodore Johnson and how many more aliases during the two-hundred years?" Hattie felt bad for having her loving husband remember such bad times, especially while he ate his dinner. "Darling, if you had rather eat your steak without all this talk about those trying times, I'll understand. I'm sure it wasn't pleasant being in that demon's company every day for that many years. William, I think you suffered far more than your family and staff did. Their suffering was cut short and their spirits appeared only during the Christmas Holly-Jolly-Getaway."

"I guess that's why I grew so bitter and..." William reached over to pinch Hattie's cheeks. "Mean, like you called me for firing Mr. Ashton without asking why when he failed to show up for work. You might have called me the town Scrooge and

I would have fit his description from the Christmas Carol!" William reached over and gave Hattie a loving kiss. "My girl saved me in every way I needed saving. You taught me to love again. To find something about myself to like. To have the strength to let go of living so that I might save others. And that which is most important, with your pure unselfish love and child-like faith, you helped saved my mortal soul by believing and trusting in me, after everything I had done to Pattie and Susanne, who had also believed my words and trusted me to always be there for them."

"Like me, Pattie and Susanne realized that you weren't yourself, not the husband and father they knew and loved. Those demons had you in some kind of trance and no matter how strong you wanted to help them get away, the demon's power over you made it impossible." Hattie felt William take her hand under the table.

"Hattie, you are right. Every time I had any thought of helping them escape, the demons appeared and I could not move. Only until the demon came out of the box in the attic and the doors and windows slammed shut permanently was I able to walk up to the house willingly. The demons knew it was too late for me to do anything to help those trapped inside. The doors were locked and my keys were missing. I never tried to find them until you came into my life and wanted to see inside the mansion."

"Let me guess who had the keys. Theodore Johnson, a thief and a murderer." Hattie made a distasteful face just remembering the rude butler. "I just pray he has not returned to Sleepy Creek in a different disguise."

"What makes you think that demon has returned to our town, Hattie?"

"I am getting too close to the truth about what he and his two helpers did to Avery Torrance and where they hid him." Hattie whispered, seeing patrons look their way.

Hattie and William strolled around in the rose garden among the lighted reindeers and giant Christmas Tree adorned with white lights. William's arm rested comfortably around Hattie's shoulders as he looked around. "Things look a lot friendlier in the garden now sweetheart than they did in 1814."

"Anytime Jesus walks among the gardens, there is a ray of his eternal love and peace, that linger for many years to come." Hattie had remembered how the light flowing from the Lamb of God, shone bright all around the grounds and manor house while he stood among them. Even after he had left with His lost sheep, Hattie could sense his presence and smell the veil of heaven being opened. "This is why I feel the appearance of Avery during the festival time is not hindered by those demons and he can freely speak to me as he recalls what happened, or to quote Mr. Torrance, what is happening." Hattie noticed William stopped with a confused look on his face. "I know, it doesn't make sense, at least not until you understand why Avery feels this way. Avery is reliving each day from December 22, 1814, til December 24, 1814, over and over each night starting at Thanksgiving, the first day of the festival. So, it is always a new day to him and he cannot tell you what will happen the next day. I feel the crucial time to find the truth will be the actual dates of December 22nd, 23rd, and 24th. If I have not found Avery Torrance by then, my hopes of finding him are gone until next season."

"I can see your dilemma Hattie darling, so if I can be of any help, please ask me anything you need." William led her to a bench and wrapped his arms around her to help keep her warm from the night chill.

"The number of chauffeurs you have had over the two-hundred-years would be a start. The names are not as important as the number, but how you came by them will be a big help." Hattie had only met Benson Edwards, the driver William had when she met him in 2014. Not wanting to change anything William had in his house when she knew him, she kept his entire staff, except of course Theodore Johnson who turned out to be a demon. Mr. Edwards had proved to be loyal and very trustworthy. "I believe Benson said he worked for you for forty years when I kept him on as my driver in 2014. He keeps in good shape and hasn't ask to be replaced so he can retire. He would be hard to replace should he want to step down."

"Benson has always done a remarkable job at both driving automobiles as well as carriages." William looked thoughtful. "I recall all of my drivers over the years carried out their jobs with dignity and never seemed to be bothered by my rude behavior. Just off the top of my head, I count six different chauffeurs, including Benson, who has been with me the longest."

"I suppose you must have lived in several states, different towns, before you came back to Sleepy Creek. I have heard grandma and mama talking about being at the town council meeting the day you came back and the Farrell sisters, June and Tracy, who own the Sleepy Creek Café and Bakery, swore you hadn't aged a bit since you came into town where they were part of the town's welcoming committee." Hattie chuckled, remembering the night William had surprised everyone in Sleepy Creek by showing up at the festival games. "Libby Fisher swore you had a face lift and I sat her straight by telling the town gossip you did no such thing!"

"I guess she finally learned the truth when my will was read." William joined Hattie in laughter. "Let's see, you wanted to know how I came by each driver." He studied the question for a while, then shook his head. "I am certain I never interviewed anyone for a job, so it must have been Johnson, who never changed his name due to the many places we lived over the two-hundred-years." William forced an I'm-sorry smile at Hattie. "I cannot recall their names either, sweetheart. I was in a bad place and it wasn't getting any easier as time crawled by. I am sure anyone who had the chance to see me after I returned would tell you I was an angry old man who hated everyone but himself. A man rarely seen by the public because I desired to stay shut away inside the rock cottage."

"I did hear people describe you that way William. Now I can see why everyone was shocked to see you talking to me in

140

the market square." Hattie recalled first meeting her William. "I was afraid of you at first. You looked so stern, never blinking as you stared down at me asking questions about my cookies."

"Then you told me the sales were for a good cause and I ask if it was for your piggy bank. That's when my little Hattie let me have it!" William laughed recalling how he started to become alive inside listening to this ten-year-old girl tell him off, never knowing she was actually talking to the owner of Marshall Mills. "Hattie, my heart was dead up until I met you. Speaking about our first meeting has made me realize why I came to the market in the first place.

I had no desire to go outside among the people of Sleepy Creek after my return. Everything seemed different and things had changed with the times except for the buildings, which remained the same as I remembered. I could not bring myself to go near the old mansion, the past still haunted me and knowing my love one's remains had to be in that old mansion someplace. So, I sat in my office, staring out the open window that I had opened to let in some cold fresh air to refresh my mind so I could concentrate on the business before me. That is when I heard your voice, calling out Hattie's-Patties, two dollars each. Something snapped inside my head and I got up and walked over to the window, hoping to hear your voice again. You repeated the words loudly. Hattie's-Patties, for two dollars and a very good cause!" William thought back, remembering walking in the entrance hall and putting on his coat, then dashing out the door before Johnson saw him and making his way to the town square. "I spotted you bending down for more cookies and walked up to your small stand, noticing you were alone."

"Wow, if you heard my voice all the way to your cottage, I guess my brothers were right calling me loud-mouth." Hattie smiled, just glad William had heard her sale's pitch.

"Hattie darling, I believe I heard you because the Lord wanted me to." William took her hand and led her to the back entrance of the B&B. "I had never had the urge to put the window up in the wintertime until that day. Its as if something told me to open my window after feeling a certain burst of hot flash come over me. I believe the Lord wanted me to meet you, even fall in love with you so you could help save me and my soul."

"And I believe our Lord knew our love for one another would grow and that is why he told me our love was meant to be, same as he told you before sending you back." Hattie followed William up to the third floor and room#6. "I wonder if Avery will show up tonight at midnight?"

CHAPTER 24

Hattie was disappointed that Avery's apparition hadn't shown up at midnight and she decided to make a quick trip into town to get her last-minute Christmas items and pay a visit to her daddy and grandpa in the market square before heading to the farm to pick up her daughter. As she was making her way across the street to Libby's Library and Book Store, she noticed the Caswell brothers watching her from the street corner. Travis Caswell tipped his hat, smiled and started walking her way, his brothers trailing behind.

"Mrs. Marshall, you seem to have your arms filled. May I be of some assistance?"

"That is very thoughtful of you Mr. Caswell, but I am accustomed of handling a great deal of packages, especially at this time of year." She had noticed earlier that a close sign had been in the window of Handyman Harvey's Hardware Store so, she felt this was a good opportunity to find out why. "Mr. Caswell, I couldn't help but notice the sign in your uncle's hardware store. With this being the busiest season in Sleepy Creek, all the stores are usually bustling with shoppers." Hattie appeared sympathetic to the men. "I am aware our friend Harvey took a bad spill a few days back, but surely no one else in your family have been hurt or became ill."

"My folks decided to close the store and head back up north to Chicago since poor unfortunate Uncle Harvey won't be able to run the store again." Travis Caswell said with a smirk. "I guess it's about time the old goat checked out."

Hattie narrowed her eyes at the uncaring man who stood blocking her way. "Mr. Caswell, I pray that you are referring to the hospital when you say it's time for Harvey to check out." Standing her ground, she pulled her bags in tightly. "If you will step aside now, I must be on my way."

The tall bully, lend back, crossing his arms, a sign of defiance. "Hattie, we will stand aside when we're good and ready."

"And, I say you had better be ready to move out of the lady's way right now!" Benson had been watching from across the narrow road where he waited next to the carriage and overheard their conversation.

The three Caswell's stared coldly at the heroic gentleman standing firmly and unafraid. "And you can make us move, sir?"

"I can and I will!" Benson stepped up in front of Hattie, towering over the tallest brother. "You have two choices gentlemen! Leave peacefully or leave on a stretcher!" The hate for the three Caswell brothers shown clearly on the driver's face as he stared, unblinking until Travis held up his hand and laughed out.

"No sweat, man! We have no fight with you, Mr. Edwards!" Travis tilted his hat at Hattie. "Just a little harmless flirting, that's all. Such a beautiful creature should never belong to just one man, a very old man at that!" A sneer fell on Travis Caswell's lips, reminding Hattie of another sneering face eleven years ago. "Miss Detective, it can be dangerous to metal into the past! It is best to forget the one left behind!" One last menacing smile, the brothers walked away laughing.

"Pay those men no mind, Hattie. They are merely trying to scare you with their insane words." Benson never took his eyes off the brothers as they continued down the sidewalk. He reached over and relieved Hattie of her packages. "Word is out that you are in search of Avery Torrance, the only staff member your Aunt Hattie failed to mention in her diary as being with those that were saved." The chauffeur walked Hattie to her parked car and placed the packages in the trunk. "Those fools have heard all the gossips offering their opinions as to what happen to Mr. Marshall's carriage driver after the rich man chose life over his family."

"Benson, who would start such a horrible story after what

William gave everyone in this town when he left with the Lord? Do those gossips not realize that if Jesus saved William, He was giving him a second chance because my darling begged for forgiveness. Susanne, Pattie and the other staff members forgave him as well." Hattie stared over at Libby's Book Store. "I can imagine who started the gossip! Those who are without sin should be the one to throw the first stone!"

"Maybe you should have a talk with your brother, who spilled the beans in the first place, trying to impress a girl he met while serving beer at the pub." Benson had overheard the conversation himself along with everyone in the bar.

"Matthew!" Hattie checked her watch, then gave Benson a grateful hug for helping her get hid of those brothers. "My darling brother is still at home, probably sleeping off the night shift. I shall drop in on daddy and grandpa later. I am headed for the Russel farm!"

"Darn Hattie, I never meant for everyone to hear what I told Goldie!" Matthew had jolted awake by the pounding on his bedroom door and his sister storming inside, demanding to know why he let the mystery out. "I tried everything to get her attention, but she ignored all my usual come-on's. When Randy Brower came in and they started talking, I had to do something to get her attention, so I blurted out, my main job is working at The Missing Piece Detective Agency with my famous sister, Hattie Russel Marshall!" Matthew swallowed as Hattie narrowed her eyes and stepped closer.

"Matthew, why didn't you simply stop at that? You know to never say anything about a case we are working on until we solve it!"

"She became so excited when I told her I was your brother! She said she was a big fan of Hattie Russel and ask what the mystery was about!" Matthew made an I'm sorry face. "I knew our missing person was a ghost from 1814 and that would make big points with the blonde bomb shell. It must have, because she grabbed me around the neck and spoke up perhaps a little too loud."

Joan Byrd

"Matthew, I hate to ask, but just what did that blonde bimbo shout out for everyone in the bar to hear?" Hattie stared down, making Matthew pull the cover up around his neck. "And do not sugar coat her words brother because Benson Edwards said he was there and heard every word."

Matthew made a sick face as he said nervously. "Goldie said, THAT'S RIGHT! HOW COULD I FORGET AVERY TORRANCE THE CARRIAGE DRIVER?" he smiled sheepishly after repeating her loud words.

"Well, Matthew Russel, I hope she made your betrayal worth it!" Hattie marched to the door. "If I see one person watching or following me while I am trying to find Avery, I will tell his wondering spirit to haunt you every night after the festival if I cannot find him!" Without another word, Hattie collected Mattie, kissed her grandmother and left for the mansion.

Strolling Mattie around in the carriage house, Hattie moved slowly past the inside walls, her hand feeling for anything suspicious. As she walked she spoke softly to Mattie, trying to piece the puzzle together. "So far I know who makes the sounds in both the library and room#6. I haven't as yet figured out how Susanne's spirit can be in the library since she left with the Lord. I discovered the missing page from Aunt Hattie's diary and know the devil was the invisible being in the rose garden on December 22nd 1814. I have come to the conclusion that the three Mr. Rockford's were really three separate demons and the leader of the group, just like Travis Caswell, was Clarence Rockford who later changed his name to Theodore Johnson. The missing Christmas card is inside Avery Torrance's vest." Hearing the side door open, Hattie turned to see Emily Torrance smiling shyly.

"I hope I am not disturbing you Hattie. I thought I might find you here and I was wondering if the news of your mystery case being leaked would affect you from finding my grandfather."

"Not in the lease. I guess you overheard my 'heated'

conversation with my big mouth brother this morning." Hattie looked apologetically down at her client. "I hope I did not wake you up. My temper got the better of me when I found out my flirty brother, Matthew, had spilled the beans just for a girl's attention."

"You did not disturb me, Hattie. I was on the phone with a friend at the time and my room is just down the hall from Matthew's." Hattie noticed the young woman's cheeks blush a bright red. "I was wondering if that invitation to the Christmas dance was still open for this evening? I know I said I had rather stay at the farm, but I thought it might be fun to invite my friend, as a date."

"A date?" Hattie suddenly was intrigued over this announcement. "Emily, you are more than welcome to come to the country club dance with a date. I'm just glad you are finally taking part in the town's activities. Will your date be anyone I know?"

Emily laughed softly. "You know him very well Hattie. I thought you might say yes so, I took the liberty this morning and called him. I've ask Benson Edwards to be my date."

"Benson?" Hattie looked surprised for a moment, never recalling seeing the chauffeur date anyone before. "Well, you both have a lot in common and I am certain Benson, with his manners and gallant charm, would make any lady feel like a princess on a date."

Emily could not control her happy emotions when she threw he arms around Hattie in a tight hug. "Oh, thank you so much! You have made me very happy!" Emily checked her watch. "I'm sorry Hattie, but I must be going! I promised Mrs. Graham, the seamstress at Fashion World I would be available at two p.m. for a fitting. See you tonight!" Before Hattie could ask if Benson would be picking her up, Emily ran from the carriage house.

"Mattie, if our carriage driver has his own date tonight, I guess this will be the first Christmas Ball the Marshall's will be driving up in the small carriage, with your daddy in the driver's seat." Hattie jumped when she heard a male laugh out.

"I never meant to frighten you Hattie but I overheard your words to little Mattie." Benson had walked in with some big silver bells and a jar of polish. "Don't you be worrying about tradition changing just because I accepted that sweet girl's invitation to the dance. I still plan to pick you and William up at the cottage as planned, the only difference is my date will be sitting next to me. I'll be picking up Miss Torrance first at the farm, then come straight to the cottage, if those plans suit you, of course."

"Benson, I could not be happier for you and Emily to enjoy a night together dancing and having a fine meal at the country club." Hattie thought a second before asking "Benson, every year since I've known you, you have stayed with the carriage while the dance is in full swing. Have you ever been inside of the country club?"

"Only to use the servant's bathroom." The driver gave her a gentle smile. "The friendly wait staff made sure the drivers always had something to eat and drink while waiting for their employers. It's really pleasant waiting outside under the stars or on a cloudy night, watching the big flakes of snow fall all around you." Benson gave a little chuckle. "I informed the young lady, when it came to dancing, I was two left feet and she assured me that might work out for us because she was two right feet."

"I know you will have fun. Just hold her in your arms and sway back and forth to the music." Hattie laughed as she recalled her first dance at the club with William when she was only ten. "It can't look no sillier than I must have looked standing on Williams's shoes in 2014."

The chauffeur pulled a stool up at an old table and began polishing the bells to tie on the horse's reins. He paused momentary, deep in thought of a time long gone. "Hattie, I must admit there was a time when I was a very fine dancer. Things were quite different back then. The dance itself was more refine and the music was both slow or smoothly fast, but the steps were the same and one could gracefully waltz around the room with your lady in toe."

"Benson, even if the years have passed away since you last danced, I just bet the music William has chosen to be played during the 1800's style Christmas dance, will have you waltzing around the ball room in no time with Emily Torrance." Hattie rolled her daughter's stroller to the open doors that face the mansion and stared out at the side entrance. She spoke softly to her daughter. "Mattie, this is where Avery watched William bring his luggage out of the house." Hattie stepped up closer and noticed she could make out the front entrance from the same big double doors. "I wonder...was Avery watching William when he left the mansion after dinner at this very same spot? Maybe he wasn't alone in the carriage house on Christmas Eve and the poor man never made it back inside before the demon in the attic sealed up the doors and windows." Hattie jumped again when she felt someone close to her and turned to see their driver staring out with her.

"So, you suspect the poor lost driver must have known too much and he was caught spying on his employer?" Benson whispered, as though he thought they might also get caught by the same ill fate of the missing chauffeur. "Who or what could have made him simply disappear and cause everyone to forget he ever existed?"

"If I tell you Benson, this can go no further until I solve the poor man's whereabouts, understood?" Hattie watched the driver nod a positive. "I have a hunch Mr. Torrance was standing at this very spot watching William leave, perhaps he even spoke softly to himself, saying something like, Mr. Marshall, just what are you up to? Avery had witnessed an obsessed man carry out bag after bag and hide them in the back of the big carriage after he had demanded his carriage driver to hook up the large carriage for him and have it brought around to the side entrance. I assume William must have moved the carriage to the front before going back inside for dinner." Hattie knew the chauffeur was taking every word in as he stared out, as though he could see everything unfolding. "I believe Mr. Rockford and his two imposters appeared in the carriage house to watch Mr. Torrance so he would not ruin their plans to shut Susanne, Pattie and the other staff members inside the mansion after William got away. I also know Rockford and the other two are fallen angels, are capable of blocking human's minds and stopping Avery somehow!"

CHAPTER 25

The dance at Marshall Country Club was going very well and everyone was dressed in 1800's attire. Hattie and William sat at their private table and watched all the guest from their spot, especially their driver and Hattie's client. Around half time William punched Hattie's arm lightly and pointed across the room. The three Caswell brothers were sitting down in the three empty chairs, obviously reserved for the night. They had no dates and looked around until they spotted Mr. Benson dancing with his date, Miss Torrance.

"Those three are probably up to no good darling." Hattie's suspicions of the three 'young' men were very strong and she did not trust them. "William, I find there is something very familiar about Travis Caswell, the oldest brother. Does he remind you of anyone you knew? Say, someone who was with you for a very long time."

William looked closer at the oldest Caswell brother and studied his face. He observed his facial emotions and instantly saw the connection between the obnoxious butler who served him for over two-hundred-years. "Hattie, there is no denying there is a similarity between the older Caswell and Rockford, alias Johnson. Are you saying they could be one in the same?"

"As of now I cannot prove my theory, but I have good reason to think all the Caswell brothers are demons." Hattie whispered, not wishing to share any information to an already growing group of amateur detectives in Sleepy Creek.

"What about Harvey's nephew, Jack Caswell? Is he a phony as well, along with Wanda?" William sipped on his wine as he kept a close watch on the three.

"I did some research on Harvey's nephew and Jack proves to be the real thing, along with his wife Wanda, but there was no sign of children by them." Hattie picked up her glass and moved in close to her husband. "I believe Jack and Wanda have been brainwashed by these demons and they believe they are their sons. I think one of the so-call brothers smashed a heavy object on the head of poor old Mr. Caswell in hopes of getting him out of the way. They made it look like a fall but the doctor in charge called me to report it was a blunt strike on his head that brought the elder Caswell man down, not a fall from the stairs as reported."

"Has the hospital reported the attempted murder to the authorities?" William glanced down at his wife whose attention was on their driver and his date.

"They had no choice but to report the attempted murder but I spoke with the police chief alone with James, our minister and informed them they could not possibly hold the Caswell's in jail because of their ability to slip out and simply disappear. It wasn't easy darling, but James and I finally convinced the 'deal with facts' police department, that these were not human men they were dealing with, but powerful fallen angels, made into demons by Lucifer." Hattie leaned up on her elbows for a better look. "We convinced them these men could cause a lot of havoc on the streets of Sleepy Creek if they knew we were on to them."

Hattie now punched her husband's arm and nodded to the men making their way to where Benson and Emily were dancing. "Hattie, I think it's time to have a dance darling." Without hesitation, William took Hattie on the dance floor and waltzed his way between the Caswell's and his driver. Marshall's eyes fell on Travis Caswell. "Gentlemen," he used the word lightly. "I see you are without a dance partner, so I suggest you either ask a lady to dance or take your seat and watch from the side."

"We must apologize Mr. Marshall. This is our first time attending your fine gala and we are not aware of the rules." Travis glanced over at Hattie and made a sweeping bow. "Begging your pardon Hattie Russel Marshall, if I could choose a perfect dance partner it would be you." He rolled his eyes to William who held her close. "Even though we are strangers in your mist, my dear, I fear your protecting husband would not permit me to have just one little dance from Sleepy Creek's most famous detective."

"Mr. Caswell, I am charmed by your gallant invitation to ask me to dance with you, but I must decline. All my dances are reserved for my beloved husband William." Hattie felt William's arms embrace her waist. "Perhaps there are some single ladies desiring some fine gentlemen, like yourself, to ask them for a dance."

Travis narrowed his eyes when William Marshall smiled and waved them back to their chairs. Before Hattie and William could return to their table, Benson Edwards stopped them.

"Mr. Marshall, Miss Torrance and I saw what you did for us and although I am very capable of handling those morons, I really appreciate knowing how much you both care about our well-being."

"Benson, you are a part of our family. We care about you and love you very much." Hattie assured the chauffeur that he was more than just an employee. "William and I did not want anything to disrupt your date with Emily. You deserve some personal happiness."

"It fills me with gratitude to know how much the two of you care." Benson smiled warmly. "To be appreciated as a person instead of just an employee is very moving."

"I have always held you with high regards Benson and although I have been well pleased with most all my drivers over the years, I felt the closest to you and Avery Torrance."

"Then I am honored to be in such gracious company, sir. "Benson smiled down to his shy date. "Miss Emily has been telling me many great things about her grandfather and I am pleased to be in the same category as him and if there is anything I can do to help you find his whereabouts, please do not hesitate to ask, Hattie."

"Thank you, Benson. I just might require your assistance in helping to locate our missing driver." The music had stopped briefly before playing 'I Only Have Eyes for You". Benson smiled broadly and motioned the couple to the dance floor. "I believe they are playing your song."

William and Hattie began dancing, blocking everyone out of their minds as the gallant husband sung the familiar words softly in the ear of the woman he loved so dearly. They were so caught up in their song, they never noticed Travis Caswell disappear and reappear in their private booth. Before the evil demon could call up a bottle of poison, Benson Edwards was there to outwit the evil man.

"Not so fast, sir. I cannot let you get away with such behavior!" The driver's eyes stared unmoving into the bad man's eyes, causing him to back away. "You have gotten by with a lot of horrible acts, Gorzar, but you will not hurt my friends!" Mr. Edwards made a step toward the evil thing. "I can tell that clever detective everything I know about you and your so-call brothers, so you had better watch your step! You can never hurt me again, so I am warning you to back off Gorzar and let Hattie Russel Marshall search for the man you made disappear over 200 years ago!"

"That smart little detective will never find Avery Torrance! We have him well hidden and her time is running out!" the demon sneered. "As for you, Benson Edwards, I hired you to be the driver for Marshall when I was acting as the wealthy man's butler, Theodore Johnson. About your getting hurt by us, I assume you are referring to our 'fixing it' so you could never please a woman and devote your entire life to being a chauffeur." A gruff laugh came from his throat. "Seeing you with such a young woman tonight was quite funny for an old man who could do no more than…kiss the fair damsel goodnight."

"Your cruel words do not hurt me anymore, Gorzar." Benson did not blink. "I have lived long enough to stop being afraid of you, even after you bragged about being a demon and telling be your real name! I will not let you hurt Hattie Russel Marshall nor will I permit you to destroy William Marshall's happiness ever again! I am living to help this girl find Avery Torrance and we both know you cannot stop me!"

"You have become too clever Edwards!" the demon snarled "It's true we cannot destroy you but we are very capable of destroying the girl and her rich husband! The little brat ruined everything! William Marshall was ours! She called on HIM to banish me from saving the demon in the box then called on the Creator again to send Worhell back to Lucifer before saving William Marshall's soul!"

"I have warned you, Gorzar! Do not go near anyone I care about! I might not know the whereabouts of Avery Torrance yet, but I swear, I will not rest until I help Hattie find his body!"

The demon laughed, then disappeared just before Hattie and William stepped back inside their private booth and found Benson Edwards staring into the space the demon had vanished.

CHAPTER 26

After explaining things to William and Hattie, the chauffeur went back to his date, knowing they would be watching their backs. The remainder of the Christmas dance went on as usual and the Marshall's felt grateful to Mr. Edwards for getting rid of the Caswell brothers.

Christmas Eve finally arrived and Hattie knew she had to prove her theory before the evening was gone or she would have to wait another year to search for the missing carriage driver. Hattie had followed Avery the previous night as he made his repeated activities for December 23rd, 1814, but December 24th was still unsure and if the carriage driver's spirit appeared at midnight, it might be too late. The brilliant detective had urged Avery Torrance to appear earlier because at the stroke of midnight it would be a new day, Christmas day.

"William, all the past appearances of Avery Torrance's ghost have been at midnight on the same day he relives them, but I feel if he waits until twelve midnight tonight, the demons will be celebrating, knowing even if he tries to relive Christmas Eve, he will be stopped and all chances of finding his body will be lost. I could sense their sureness that it would be impossible for his spirit to show me what happened to him. Up until now, Dec. 24th is the only day I have witnessed only once, and Avery changed things then."

"So, this is why you insisted we leave your family's Christmas Eve celebration early tonight." William held her in his embrace, afraid of what might happen if Avery's ghost did show up and she would be confronted by the three demons that hid him for all these years. "Hattie, I wished there was some way I could travel back with you to 1814. I would die if you disappeared along with my faithful carriage driver."

"William, I believe I have come up with the reason why we

can hear the spirit of not only Avery, but Susanne in our time. How I could see you my love in the 1814 rose garden."

"Hattie darling, are you saying you know why the Claxton's could hear noises obviously made by Avery Torrance, since it was his bedroom and Andrew and some other guest heard footsteps in the library, a woman's and a man's, then sounds coming from the desk in the corner? The reason you saw me?"

"William, I cannot prove it just yet but when I find Avery Torrance, then I will be certain." Hattie laid her head on his shoulder. "All I can tell you right now is these sounds are not made by ghost hauntings. Susanne's spirit lives in heaven so that would make it impossible. I have read about these, strange occurrences called phenomena. It has been described as a hologram, a life-giving force and the trauma caused by those who appear at the same time every year are merely reflections from the past."

"Darn Hattie, how on earth did you figure that up?" William shook his head, amazed.

Hattie gave him a beautiful smile. "I am just a great detective Mr. Marshall. If things go the way I have planned tonight, I will know how to locate our missing carriage driver."

"As long as there is no chance of your getting hurt from these plans, then I pray they work and that devoted man can at last find peace."

Hattie was awakened at ten p.m. by Avery Torrance's spirit and she found herself inside the carriage house as the sun from Christmas Eve, 1814 was setting in the west. She was standing next to the carriage driver as he stood waiting just inside the carriage house's double doors.

"Mr. Marshall should be coming out any time now. The poor man looks so disturbed over what he is planning to do, but I feel those demons have him blocked." Avery pulled out his pocket watch and checked the time. "Almost eight. The Marshall family eat exactly at seven so he should be coming out any moment."

The front door opened and William walked out speaking to someone just inside the door. "Susanne, I promise to return in plenty of time to take you and Pattie to the church services at nine. Just be ready." The nervous man climbed up on the carriage and drove away. Avery Torrance stared at him as he made his way quickly down the driveway and out of sight.

"William Marshall, just what are you up to?" then he heard the familiar voice behind him.

"Mr. Torrance, did I not warn you about getting too nosy?"

Hearing the distinguish voice behind him, Avery knew immediately who was waiting behind him and his main thoughts were on saving Hattie Russel. He quickly opened a secret panel in front of him and shoved her inside.as he whispered.

"Stay hidden! They have not seen you yet." Pressing a button, the wall slid back in place as he turned to watch the three demons surround him.

"Torrance, who were you whispering to just now?" Clarence Rockford breathed down on him. "This is something new."

"I am aware of my fate this time Rockford! I am also aware of the fact that you will not physically hurt me. Your goal is to rob any chance that I might have to leave this world and go on to heaven. To make my poor spirit wonder through the halls of the mansion, carriage house and stables for all eternity." The carriage driver showed the three demons no fear, most likely from the long period of time he had endured their evil presence. "I was merely whispering to myself the words you would be repeating. The same words, over and over again! Torrance, I warned you about getting too nosy! Now, you must face a long future of repeated work! Never to stop toiling, throughout eternity!" Avery Torrance spoke loud enough for Hattie to hear his words. "I also know you have blocked everyone's memory of me as well as blocking my own memory as to where I will go from here! I am only aware of the tormented nights between Thanksgiving, 1814 and December 24th, 1814. All else is wiped from my memory."

"Very clever Mr. Torrance." The head demon sneered. "And that is where you will remain, once and for all! There is one lassie who lives far ahead in the 2000's who is in search of your whereabouts, but she is not as smart as she thinks she is." Rockford, alias Johnson gave a loud wicked laugh, followed by his silent companions. "Soon Christmas day will be here and her time for finding you will run out!" the demon moved in close and looked around the driver, sensing a presence nearby. Hattie stood quietly, trying not to make a sound as she held her breath in the very tight compartment, too small for a man.

"I do not think you are as certain about this lassie's capabilities in finding me, Rockford, as you claim!" Avery chuckled and pulled his watch from his vest pocket. "You must be unsure of her talents or you would not be here early." The driver smiled when they mumbled to one another. "That's right, you showed up an hour early so I still have one hour before I go to that place of forgetfulness."

"Enjoy your measly little hour Torrance!" Rockford bellowed and turned to leave shouting back. "That girl will waste her time searching your cottage for you. Look for our return in exactly fifty-nine minutes!"

CHAPTER 27

"I heard everything you said to that demon Avery." Hattie had slipped back out when the carriage driver opened back the pandal. "Our time has almost run out so I just need to ask you a couple of questions to verify my theory for solving your whereabouts. I am well aware I will not find you behind that panel."

"Nor in the cottage, according to Rockford. But you think you know where my body is Hattie?" Avery asked anxious as he kept his eyes peered on the back door.

"Yes Avery, I am more than certain." Hattie knew time was ticking as she asked. "Avery, you said you always keep the Christmas card on you at all times."

"Yes ma'am!" he patted his vest pocket.

"Avery, did Charlotte have perhaps a middle name?" Hattie bit her lip after she asked Avery to check his pocket watch and found out she had only thirty minutes left.

"Charlotte was my beautiful wife's middle name. Her first name was Emily. Emily Charlotte Torrance." He smiled just saying his true love's name.

"Would you describe Emily Charlotte to me?"

"My beloved Charlotte was a petit blonde with the most beautiful blue eyes I have ever seen." Avery thought back to happier times. "I first met my beloved at a dance. I never considered myself a good dancer but when Emily Charlotte was in my arms, I felt like I was floating on air." Tears came to the devoted man's eyes. "I had promised her so many things like our new home and the fact that we would be together in the springtime. For some unseen reason, I ended my last letter to her with something like, never forget, Christmas is a time for miracles and then on her Christmas card I keep next to my heart, the words, love comes at Christmas!" Hearing a sound

The Missing Christmas Card

near the back door and sensing the demons near, he gave Hattie a hug as he whispered. "I am sending you back now. I pray that I will see you over my spirit tomorrow, Christmas day and this will be over." With love in his eyes he said softly. "Thank you, Hattie Russel Marshall. I love you, my very special friend. Goodbye."

"I love you too Avery Torrance and keep the faith, this is not goodbye. It is only a new beginning!" Hattie reached up to kiss his cheek and smiled at the surprised demons before disappearing.

Hattie came down the stone cottage stairs singing Joy to the World, reached up and kissed her husband, before dancing to the kitchen. William followed behind her smiling happily, carrying their little girl who cradled her new baby doll in her arms.

"Hattie, my darling, you either got what you ask Santa to bring you or you have solved the mystery of Avery Torrance." He sat Mattie in her highchair and grabbed Hattie up in his arms. "Care to fill your partner in, Mrs. Marshall?"

"Let me just say, Christmas is a time for miracles!" Hattie laughed happily. "As my time was running out last night, the last piece of the puzzle fell magically into place. I had my suspicions about the outcome but after hearing Avery's words to that demon Rockford, I was totally convinced!"

"Hattie, you where there with those three demons?" William suddenly grew tense.

"Avery knew more than most ordinary ghost and he cleverly hid me from their sight." She giggled "The demons sensed my presence but your clever carriage driver diverted their attention from finding my hiding place. A very tiny opening behind a secret panel. He is such a clever man."

"Hattie, my love, you speak as though the dear man is still alive." William unsure of his wife's big grin, narrowed his eyes. "Are you referring to his ghost being a clever man?"

"My persistent charming husband, you shall know soon enough." Hattie handed him a hot cup of coffee, stirred with the perfect amount of cream and sugar he loved and made her way to the door. "I'm off to get ready for our Christmas day celebration with the Russel family. Starting with grandma's special Christmas brunch! I hope Benson has the carriage all ready to head out to Russel farm!" Hattie walked away singing: Dashing through the snow in a four-horse open sleigh…"

"Merry Christmas Benson! I see you are all dressed for the season." Hattie smiled as he helped her up.

"Yes ma'am, dressed in my Christmas attire." He titled his hat to his employer. "Mr. Marshall, a Merry Christmas to you and your lovely family sir."

"Benson, I do not know how my darling Hattie talked you into driving us to the farm this morning after I gave you the day off, but I appreciate it and all you do for us." William had expected to take the smaller carriage out to the farm himself and was surprised when Hattie had mentioned the carriage driver being ready to drive out to the Russel farm.

"Driving the carriage gives me a warm feeling Mr. Marshall and to be frank, it gives me something to do today besides sat around inside my lonely apartment rooms playing Christmas Carols and trying to remember what I have done besides drive a carriage."

"Then it's settled. You will be spending Christmas with the Russel's, Benson." Hattie glanced at William and noticed his wink, so she continued. "It will never do for anyone to spend Christmas day by themselves when there are those who love you."

"Such a gracious invitation should never be turned down, so I except it with a joyful heart." Benson gave a happy click of his tongue and the horses started off in a trot up the steep hill, through the streets of Sleepy Creek and continued until the carriage reached the country road leading to the Russel Farm.

Inside the farmhouse, after everyone extended loving hugs and kisses, the Marshall's settled down by the warm fire, Mr. Edwards right across from them. Hattie waited until she noticed a bead of sweat trickled down the carriage driver's face before standing up, arms extended in front of her.

"Benson, please let me take you coat and hang it up." Hattie turned to her husband. "I will take yours too darling. I think this warm fire has warmed our cold body's by now and you know how hot the family room gets with all the Russel's opening their presents." The men could not resist Hattie's beautiful smile as they both stood and removed their long wool winter coats. She noticed Benson pull down on his old warn vest and smiled to herself.

"Benson, that must be a special vest you're wearing. It looks very old. Wouldn't you agree William?"

"It does look like something out of the 1800's." William walked over to have a closer look. "I could swear I have seen this vest someplace before." His eyes fell over on Hattie, who was smiling. "Is it a vest I have seen before, darling?"

"Why don't you ask Benson, William." Hattie casually took her seat and gave him a knowing smile. "You must have seen it on him many past Christmas Holidays."

"Hattie is right sir. I am sure you have seen me wear this vest ever since I was hired to be your driver." Benson glanced over at a smiling Hattie. "I have worn it every Christmas for as long as I remember."

"You and all of my other drivers over the years." William looked perplexed as Hattie pulled him down next to him.

"And there is a very good explanation as to why you remember seeing all those other drivers wear Benson's lovely old vest." Both men looked at the smart detective, each one needing to know what she knew that they did not. "Benson, the reason you remember wearing this very old vest for as long as you remember, is because, you have worn it for over two-hundred-years and counting."

"Over two-hundred-years?" The driver could not resist his chuckle. "I beg your pardon ma'am, but that would make me a very old man and I am…" Benson glanced down embarrassed. "Begging your pardon, Mr. &Mrs. Marshall, I lied about my age when I was first hired. I simply cannot remember how old

Joan Byrd

I really am or when I was born."

"At this moment, you are forever 29 years old but in reality, you are 240 years old." Hattie and William jumped up to grab the swaying driver and help him in a chair. "I am really sorry if I have shocked you, but soon you will remember who you are and it will make this revelation worth the sudden anxiety."

"The demons did the same thing to Avery Torrance when they made me live for over 200 years!" William finally recognized the missing carriage driver. "This is why we never found any signs of his body! He has been alive the entire time!"

"But unlike your case, William darling, the demons took Avery's memory away as to who he was, except when they cursed his spirit to leave his body while he slept between Thanksgiving and December 24th and sent him back in time to relive three days, over and over for over 200 years." Hattie kneeled down in front of the troubled man and took his hands.

"Avery, there is a secret pocket inside your vest where you kept very personal things. Think Avery! Try to remember the very important thing that has been missing for as long as you have."

His hand went straight to the pocket over his heart as tears swelled up in his eyes. "I remember placing a Christmas card in there. A very special card for...Charlotte! My dearest love." His sad eyes looked into Hattie's. "If it is...2025?" Avery dropped his head in Hattie's lap and wept.

"Avery, remember what you wrote in Charlotte's letter. Christmas is a time for miracles. Your words last night convinced me that my theory was right and the first miracle is we found you. Now we can free you from the demon's curse and you will be able to be with your Charlotte."

"Jesus came back for Susanne, Pattie and all my staff family, my dear friend Lucas." Avery sat up, hope reflecting on his handsome face at last. "I know the Lord forgave you Mr. Marshall and took you to heaven and..." Avery Torrance stopped and looked again into his happy employer's face. "He sent you back to Hattie! Love comes at Christmas!"

The Missing Christmas Card

Hattie and William watched Avery pull the old Christmas card from his pocket and kiss it, looking upward. "Charlotte, I wish you could see your Christmas card darling. It is as perfect as you are."

"Avery, I have waited a very long time to hear you say that!" everyone turned to see the petit blonde with blue eyes standing on the stairsteps. I was hoping you would recognize me when we danced at the Christmas ball."

"Emily Charlotte!" Avery stood up and walked quickly to the steps. "My dearest, it has been many years since we danced at the Christmas Ball. You were a stranger to me but I knew the moment I took you into my arms that we were one."

William leaned over to his wife and whispered. "Hattie, what is his granddaughter doing? Surely she is not leading on her own grandfather."

"Sweetheart, you can relax. After questioning the 1814 Avery Torrance, I realized this was not his granddaughter so I did some research late last night and found out that Evan Torrance, Avery's only son, had all girls so the Torrance name stopped with him." Hattie smiled warmly at the loving couple. "Darling, our loving Savior has blessed another beautiful couple with another chance to live again and spend their life together."

"Another Christmas miracle!" William took around his wife.

"A Christmas miracle where love comes at Christmas!" Hattie pulled her coat from the closet and handed William his. "Now to go spread a little Christmas jeer to the newest family in Sleepy Creek and free Avery from their curse!"

"The Caswell brothers?" William stopped to listen to Avery's words to his wife Charlotte and smiled to himself as he followed Hattie out to the family's old truck. "We are taking the truck?"

"The demons won't be expecting a truck but a fancy carriage." Hattie laughed as she climbed behind the wheel and took the keys from the ash tray. "Let's go give those charming men a Christian farewell!"

165

Joan Byrd

CHAPTER 28

The Marshall's walked up quietly to Harvey Caswell's dwelling and peeked inside the window. They recognized the leader of the group immediately. Only this time Travis Caswell resembled Theodore Johnson. Hattie glanced up at her husband and made a distasteful face.

"The not-so-charming Mr. Johnson. Your long-time butler."

"Hattie, we can't just walk in and confront those demons on our own." William gripped her hand in his. "They are more powerful than they appear. Remember what they did to me and Torrance."

"William darling, we won't be walking inside alone, I promise." Hattie smiled reassuringly "At this very moment the Holy Creator has sent us three very powerful angels of our own to confront their evil fallen brothers. I can assure you the Lord Himself will appear to end their presence with us from now on." She reached up and touched his face. "William darling, just remember your walks with Jesus in heaven and the Christmas miracle he gave us. Just believe!"

"Let's do this!" William stood straight as he opened the door and shouted, "Merry Christmas!"

The demons jumped at the abrupt entrance and was taking back momentary before regaining their cunning smiles. "Well now, just the two we knew would be coming by to see us." The head demon had quickly changed back to the young man. "Tell me, Miss detective, how does it feel to lose a case?"

"I would not know, Mr. Caswell. I have never lost a single case yet!" Hattie noticed all the demons narrow their eyes. The leader suddenly laughed. "So, the Christian girl is not above lying?"

"I have never told a lie either sir, unlike you." Hattie

166

stopped smiling and stared into the leader's eyes. "Everyone knows Harvey Caswell did not fall from the stairs. One of you evil brothers hit the poor man over the head, attempting to kill him."

"Attempting? You mean the old fool survived the...Fall?" the leader snarled.

"Harvey is doing very well, thank you! He was released from the hospital over a week ago." She knew their next question, so she jumped back in. "And before you ask, he is safe with friends. He would never return to his home as long as the three of you jackals are living in his house!"

"You really do think you're smart, don't you Hattie Russel Marshall?" the leader turned quickly on William. "And you, being sent back from the same place we were!"

"I was sent back to live my life a new with the ten-year old girl I fell in love with when you made yourself my tormenter for over two-hundred-years! Now you go as Travis Caswell, but in the 1800's you went as Clarence Rockford, my butler, then switched to Theodore Johnson, the terrible!"

"Both of you appear so clever but you are both fools to try and take on three powerful angels!" the leader yelled "I still have Avery Torrance Hattie Russel Marshall and all your fancy words will never change that fact nor will you find him, ever!"

"That is where you are wrong, Gorzar! This very smart young lady has more intelligence in her little finger than you have in your entire wicked body!" Avery had saw the couple slip out and followed them on Matthew's motorcycle. "When you saw her briefly last night before I sent her back to the future, she had put the missing pieces together and learned the truth. How you kept hiring me over and over, making me believe I was someone different each time. So, sure of yourself, told me your real name!"

"Alright, the clever detective may know you are still alive but she does not have the power to stop your spirit from traveling back to the past ever Thanksgiving to relive your last three days of 1814 over and over again!" the angry demon stepped up close to Hattie, only to get knocked back by an unseen force.

Suddenly the room was lit up in a bright glow as three radiant angels appeared. "Gorzar, Zansor, I see you are still doing Lucifer's bidding. I guess you will never learn that good always conquers hate and evil." The center angel's voice was silky smooth as he faced the demons unafraid. "You shall never have enough power to win over the Almighty God. Can you not remember it was I that tossed you out of heaven and into the deep below before sending the powerful Lucifer behind you?"

"It is impossible to forget you, Michael! You could have chosen our side and become Lucifer's next in line, but you chose bowing down to the Creator, so now I have that status." Gorzar sneered. "I put the curse on this man and it shall stay in place!"

"I cannot imagine ever going against the Lord God who deserves all my praises and loyalty." Michael glanced over at the man who had claimed to be Tank Caswell. "And you, Lucifer, letting your servant do all your speaking as you size up those standing in front of you. You failed with Worhell after making him a hideous monster to torture nine innocent people he had locked away for 200 years. You will fail with Avery Torrance as well!"

"You may be able to undo the spell placed on this nosy carriage driver, but you cannot erase the years of his life." Lucifer gave a sick laugh. "Too bad JESUS sent back his wife so they might have a life together." The devil's red eyes moved to Hattie and William. "Much like he did for these two. Such a beautiful Christmas miracle." Satan laughed loudly, causing an echo to bounce around the room. "LOVE! It will buy you nothing! Mrs. Torrance will be left alone again when I reverse the life spell and Avery Torrance will be nothing but a pile of dust!"

"My son, love is a beautiful and perfect thing because it flows from the Father, to the Son, then to the Holy Spirit." As the warm words flowed, the image of a man wearing a white robe appeared and everyone in the room recognized the Son of God. Lucifer and the other two fallen angels backed away. "My children, you knew only love and yet, the gift of choice given to every angel created, both big and small, was your undoing. You sought the impossible Lucifer! There is nothing that can take the place of the Holy Trinity. You are a creation made by the creator but somewhere bedded down deep inside you, you became vain and filled with jealousy and envy. You were created to be the angel of light, forever, special and powerful. The most beautiful angel in all creation and your destination began your desolation!" Jesus was filled with compassion for the lost angels who had chosen their own fate. "Even now you think you can remove this poor man from the earth, the same earth the Father, Holy Creator created, and allows you to serve on with you evil misguidance toward His children, my people! I have come for two reasons, Lucifer. To remove the unwanted years from Avery Torrance's life and return him to twenty-nine-years-of age, same as he was when you interfered with my child. William Marshall! The second reason for my presence is my abandoning you and your demons from this small town for as long as this earth remains!" Jesus held out his hands and shouted, "BE GONE SATAN AND YOU DEMONS OF THE UNDER WORLD!" in a flash, they were gone and Avery Torrance could feel the gift of new life flowing into his body and soul. "Now, my son, you are made whole, filled with the LIVING WATER! Love always comes at Christmas, for I am love! "Jesus stepped up to Hattie and William, giving her a wink.

"I can see love radiates from you both. I was watching the night you came back William and I could not resist making you drop your tray of cookies Hattie, so you could look up to find your William just as you saw him at ten years old."

"You wouldn't be responsible for starting the music would you, Lord?" Hattie beamed with total joy.

"I can see your gift for detective skills are working like we planned before creation." Jesus laughed softly when Hattie's mouth fell open, then gave her a hug. "I shall be sure I send all the impossible cases to you, Hattie Russel Marshall." With those words, a bright light filled the room and the Lord was gone, taking the angels with him.

After spending a happy celebration with the family, Hattie, Mattie and William were driven back to the stone cottage, sitting wrapped together in the back seat of the large carriage. Avery and Charlotte felt like newlyweds as they rode up front, sitting close together still madly in love after 211 years apart.

William Marshall smiled to himself as he recalled the words he heard spoken between them and he knew how to make that dream come true. He felt very pleased that Hattie had not heard their words so she too would be surprised when he revealed the gift the Marshall's would be giving his loyal driver and his wife.

Avery Torrance helped Hattie down before taking little Mattie from her daddy and handing her to the bright detective. As William climbed easily down on his own, Avery lovingly lifted his petite wife down and stole a quick kiss.

"Avery, I cannot tell you and Charlotte just how happy I am for you both. To be separated for all these years and finally have another chance to be together is something we share with you." Hattie gave them a warm hug. "My years without William were short compared to yours but your love for each other is as perfect as the day you left your family Avery and came to Sleepy Creek."

"And because your faith never wavered the entire time you remained alive never remembering who you really were except when your spirit left your body while you slept from Thanksgiving until Christmas Eve, our beautiful loving Savior rewarded the love that was cut short by his once beautiful angel, Lucifer." William pulled Hattie over and lifted little Mattie up in his strong arms and cradled her next to his side so he could wrap his free arm around the young woman he loved. "Avery, I know I usually give you a Christmas bonus as your gift, but this year I think you deserve something very special." William's eyes met Hattie's and he could read total love looking back. William knew he had her blessing for whatever he intended to give this devoted couple.

"Avery, you and Charlotte had a dream over 200years ago, to have your own cottage on the grounds of the Marshall estate." William squeezed Hattie's hand as he continued. "I was the one responsible for ruining those dreams as well as destroying not only my family, and the house servant's future but yours, as well. I cannot undo what I have done, but I can help make new dreams come true for two deserving people. I managed to sneak away from the gift unwrapping ceremony today and call the same architect, who is staying at the William and Hattie Hotel, my wonderful wife called when she had the mansion made into a bed and breakfast, Mr. Bill Claxton, master builder from McDowell County. I had my secretary to fax him your cottage plans from the 1800's and he has promised to start work on January 2nd. William turned to his wife, who had tears in her eyes, so proud of her thoughtful loving husband. "There is more, Hattie darling."

"More?" Hattie looked up and wondered what possibly could match giving the Torrance's their dream home together at last."

"For starters, the cottage has been promised to be finished by springtime so your words to Charlotte can come true. Do you remember your words?" William smiled, recalling their conversation.

"Like I wrote it yesterday." Avery took his wife's hands. "Hope blooms in the springtime!"

"Hope comes from God, so he has made sure this cottage will be made ready by Spring." William couldn't resist a chuckle, recalling Andrew's words to him while the family cheered for every open gift. "Andrew and I had a long conversation during the gift exchange, and the first thing he told me was he had noticed the path that led to the old cottage was clean and looking like new, not a weed in sight. He said he could not resist going down the path to see if anything else had changed and was overwhelmed to learn the old ruin was standing tall so he tried the door but found it locked. He peeked inside the window and noticed there was still a few unfinished rooms. The only one capable of doing this miracle is?"

"Our Lord!" Hattie laughed joyfully. "Now I can understand how Mr. Claxton can finish by the spring!" She threw her arms around her husband. "And I know where the key is?"

"You know where that old key got to?" William smiled.

"Remember darling, I found the old key in one of Susanne's secret drawers in her desk and Avery's spirit told me it belonged to the cottage door." Hattie winked at the carriage driver. "You will find it tucked away in his vest pocket. Probably deep down inside it."

"I was wondering what that hard thing was I kept feeling from the outside." The driver carefully placed his fingers inside the fragile old garment and pulled out the solid brass key. "It will almost be the same as it was in 1814, except the mansion will no longer have just one family."

"That is my other surprise." The nanny came out and got the yawning little girl to get ready for bed as William thanked her, he gathered his wife in his arms. "This is my Christmas present to you, Hattie. You know how we have talked about a house full of children and tried to make the cottage work out with those plans. Andrew has helped me decide what we should do to correct those problems. Your brother has been taking divinity studies on the internet and has completed his final test to become the new Methodist Minister in Sleepy Creek. I will be giving Andrew and Shannon's family the stone cottage, for they have decided to stop at two children."

"You have given Andrew and Shannon...our home?" Hattie could not wrap her mind around his decision without asking her first. "But William, all our memories are here, in this home!"

"It isn't a done deal yet precious." William touched her

beautiful sad face. "Just hear me out before you say no, darling."

"I trust your judgment, William, so please help me understand why you want to move us out." Hattie had tears in her eyes.

"Precious, the stone cottage holds beautiful memories for both of us and I would never just give it away without a plan." William never liked to see his girl cry so he knew his words would make her feel better. "I have merely loaned your brother and Shannon the cottage until their house is completed near the church. The old parsonage needs a lot of work and I've promised Jim, he and Ester need not move after he retires. I am going to help him restore it." William's lips met Hattie's smiling lips. "The cottage will always be our little getaway my love but the mansion on the hill will once again become the Marshall Mansion and a replica of the Marshall Bed & Breakfast will be built across town on the opposite hill. I have already giving Bill Claxton the original plans of the 1800's mansion and he said restoring it back to the way it was would be a pleasure."

"William, I must admit the mansion will hold a lot more, little Marshall's running around." Hattie laughed, recalling the difference between the mansion and the rock cottage. I hope the bed and breakfast is ready by next Thanksgiving for the regular guest."

"I can guarantee all the jobs will be completed before the Holly Jolly Getaway festival begins next season." William chuckled. "Our friend Claxton says he can hire a lot of extra help. The master quarters will be the only rooms to change in the mansion. This is William and Hattie's Mansion now, and new memories can be written in that little diary of yours!"

"So, until the first of the year, the cottage will be filled with our love and our small staff will continue to serve our needs, but once we make the big move, we will have to triple our loyal workers." Hattie smiled over at her dear friend Avery. "But we will never outgrow the need for just one carriage driver, Avery."

Joan Byrd

"It will seem like old times, working at the mansion instead of downtown." He glanced down at his smiling wife. "Only this time, my life will move forward and Charlotte will be by my side."

"Merry Christmas, dear friend." Hattie hugged him and gathering William's hand, walked inside their warm and charming cottage. Avery laughed out when he heard the young women say. "Racing Reindeer! We have got to start watching for that jolly old fat elf next Christmas Eve and see which fireplace he chooses to drop down in our very large new home! Little Mattie will be anxious about which chimney Santa decides to come down if we do not put out all the fires burning in all the mansion's fireplaces!" Hattie laughed when William chuckled and watched her reach for a small box and handed it to her husband. "Merry Christmas sweetheart. I hope you like it."

Watching her bright smile, William Marshall knew it was something special. "It's too small for a painting." He winked at her, recalling the picture she had drawn of the two of them when she was only ten years old. He opened the box and his eyes grew wide as he read the card showing a baby in blue. "Merry Christmas daddy, you have a boy!" William, grabbed her up into his arms laughing before they got down on the floor. After spending all Christmas day finally solving the mystery about Avery Torrance disappearance, watching with delight the three evil angels being sent away from Sleepy Creek forever and witnessing another Christmas miracle, Hattie and William finally found time to help Santa put Mattie's new doll house together, shaped like the cottage. This turned out to be another wonder Christmas in Sleepy Creek. A Christmas of miracles! For Avery and his Charlotte, new hope blooming in the springtime and the beautiful gift of LOVE! LOVE ALWAYS COMES AT CHRISTMAS! Jesus smiled down, His spirit singing:
"FOR I AM LOVE!"

AUTHOR'S NOTES

I hope you have had the chance to read BOOK # 1, THE BOX IN THE ATTIC before reading BOOK # 2, THE MISSING CHRISTMAS CARD. If you did, you would have been blocked from remembering the Marshall's servant who was left behind. Even I had my memory blocked by my very charming and intelligent guardian angel, Patrick. After revealing to me he deliberately had one of the servants missing from the mansion when Hattie Russel went inside to save those trapped, I was totally dumbfounded. I started trying to guess who I had forgotten and when he told me I grabbed my mouth in surprise.

Angels can do things humans could never do. Besides flying, they can breathe under water, which explains how the fallen angels could survive in the deep which is now earth. They can block your memory. The very thing Patrick did to me when I was small and could see him and speak to him. He informed me he blocked himself from me so I could grow up and live my life without depending on him, until such time he would revile himself to me again. That time came when he said, "Get your books out!"

Angels can do a great deal more things we cannot do, but a guardian's first responsibility is to protect and guide their ward throughout his or her life. The almighty God pairs you up when He creates your spirit (soul) in heaven, then places that little soul into your mother's womb. Patrick has been with me from my beginning and we are very close. I thank the good Lord for Patrick every day!

You too have a guardian angel. Give them a word of thanks, even if you cannot hear or speak in spirit.

COMING

Hattie Russel Marshall receives a mysterious message from the past, placed inside a very old bottle, trapped beneath the frozen waters of Sleepy Creek.

Somewhere just outside the town of Sleepy Creek stands an old, forgotten, run-down mansion whose faded sign reads, "The Holly Hill Inn, Your Christmas Getaway!"

What past dangers lie ahead for the bright detective as she solves another Christmas mystery from the past?

Book #3: *The Last Christmas Visitor at Holly Hill Inn*